"Entertaining and insightful – a new writer to celebrate."
CHRIS VAN WYK, author of *Shirley, Goodness and Mercy*

"Succeeds brilliantly in documenting the painful exploration of a daughter losing a mother . . . "
SAMANTHA PAGE, *O Magazine*

"Reads more like a well-crafted memoir than a novel. It gets under your skin as only a simple story well told can."
MARGIE ORFORD, *Sunday Times*

"A well-woven pastiche of memory and forgetting . . . sensitively taking the reader on the ultimate journey that we must all face . . ."
JENNIFER CROCKER, *Cape Times*

"A poignant, compelling tale that reads simply and effortlessly, yet packs in a world of detail. Beautiful . . . it marks the emergence of an exciting new talent."
LAURA MELVILLE, *The Witness*

"An excellent first novel, easy to read, yet informative and filled with emotion."
LESLEY GORE, *Books & Leisure*

"It will no doubt leave you fondly recalling family memories of your own . . . a story about compassion, love and bereavement."
KIM SHAW, *Style*

"Poignant . . . you'll find yourself wanting to find out more."
Drum

"A beautiful, sensitive look at family relationships."
Shape

After the dust has settled
on the clean rings
where tables and chairs
once stood,
and family portraits
of happier times
are taken down,
leaving chips
in the plaster
and holes in the wall,
here our ghosts
will twist and dance.
– *Dissolution*

Break the silence

I am tired. Only coffee and cigarettes are keeping me going, and I quit smoking more than five years ago. Suddenly, my phone rings and I stare at it silently without answering. You know what it's like when you get that call late at night. You hesitate, knowing that it can only be bad news, but you answer it anyway.

So, before the phone goes to voicemail, I answer. Listen softly; exhale. Wrong number. Part of the risk you take when you leave your phone on all night.

I look at my sister, Lili, dozing on the leatherette chair opposite me. Undisturbed by the shriek of the phone. I half wonder how she can sleep. For a moment, I almost envy her.

We are sitting in a room in a hospital. And what we are waiting for is news of our mother. It is no longer whether she will live, but when the end will come. Of course the doctors do not say this to us, but I can see it in their eyes. And in the averted eyes of the nursing staff who are helpful and not at all like the newspaper horror stories about nurses in state hospitals.

I feel as if the roof is coming down on me, the room closing in. It is not a decorated room. A collection of odd chairs are scattered about,

cluttering the tiny room with their bulk; a chipboard square masquer-
ades as a table. No windows, nothing to look out at, no pretty curtains.

Worn magazines, filled with last year's gossip, hold no appeal. There
is an abandoned takeout carton on a metal fold-up chair. Chinese food,
I assume from the residue of oil clinging to the bottom of the container.
Probably left over by the last occupants of this room.

Who can eat in a place like this?

Eventually I decide to go outside for another cigarette. I can concentrate on that: the inhale and the exhale. Maybe then, for the few
minutes it takes me to finish the cigarette, I can forget that inside, my
mother is dying.

I now know that hospitals provide the families of the dying with
rooms where they can be alone. We close the door behind ourselves
when we enter, but all the room affords us is privacy. It is no refuge. I
know that we can smoke here, because there is a not-quite-clean ashtray on the table. Still, I prefer going outside, even though it means a
long walk through the twisting wards.

There is another family as stricken as we are, hovering in the lobby
outside the wards. There are so many signs – things that we noticed,
yet only realised the meanings of later. Things we know but do not talk
about. Like the ominous moving to a private ward so that the family
can sit with the patient in peace, without being disturbed. So that death
does not disturb the other patients or their visitors.

The well-meaning visitors of the other patients hover at the entrance to the private ward. They smile sheepishly and press my shoulder, as if I am the kind of person who enjoys that sort of thing. They mumble their shames and say things like, "She's going to a better place . . ."

Such is the familiarity of death.

The frantic activity, the foetid smell masked by antiseptics and the unnaturally bright lights trigger my memory. Against my will, I recall another night, another waiting room; the same fear that my mother was dying.

But that was so long ago. I have forced myself to forget that time, so that now it surfaces only in the restlessness of dreams. And although the dreams have tapered off over the years, that fear never completely leaves.

Now I find myself having to confront my dream. Face my fears head-on, as the TV talk-show hosts and self-appointed life coaches like to preach to the lonely, the lost. Yet I know that whatever happens, I will be okay. I am a survivor.

I enter the room silently. As I click the door closed, Lili shifts on the tacky yellow leatherette chair on which she has managed to fall asleep, curled up in a foetal position, somehow able to appear graceful. Although it's the kind that is longer than it is wide, I am certain that sleep would elude me on such a chair.

My sister is elegantly dressed. That is just the way she is. We live so far apart, yet we are close. She is a consultant to a large multinational, based in London. Aware that she's been having a hard time at work, I've tried to shelter her from all of this. Over the phone, I have been vague and optimistic. Looking at her in that uneasy space between awake and asleep, I suddenly feel overwhelmingly protective towards her, even though she is older than me.

The chair is obviously not comfortable. Lili stirs some more. She starts to make those waking-up noises she used to make when she was a young girl. I used to think her mewling sounds theatrical; now I realise that theatrics would not have lasted this long.

Awake now, she frowns at me. Then she realises where she is and why she is here and goes into the efficient mode that has served her so well in her career. "Is everything okay?" she asks tentatively.

"No change," I offer, not sure what to say.

The distance between us stretches into an uncomfortable silence, heightened by our surroundings, our circumstances, our ghosts.

"Do you remember that time?" I venture bravely. It comes to me that maybe if we can say all the things we have not said, then maybe it will be easier – easier than feeling this fresh wound on old scar tissue.

Lili stares at me blankly, as if to ask what the hell I'm talking about. But she knows.

"The first time?" she says, then looks away. Closes her eyes.

"That time in the hospital . . ."

Are you having a bad day?

It is past three on a Wednesday afternoon; I am struggling to come up with ways to describe my client's latest innovation in skincare when the phone rings, interrupting my train of thought. I answer politely, veiling my irritation.

"Oh, it's you," I say when my mother tentatively says my name.

"Hello to you too, Sunshine," she answers. Before I can respond, she asks, "Can you come for lunch on Sunday?"

"I'll see," I mutter, my eyes not leaving my computer screen. Each time I realise that I have made a false start, I delete everything. The blank screen a silent reproach.

"No, you must come, Danika!"

Her unexpected use of my first name alerts me to the purpose in her voice.

"I can't talk now," I tell her, "but I will come, okay?"

"Fine," she says after the merest sigh. "I'll see you then. Don't be late!"

Alison, the art director I work with, looks at me, her brows raised quizzically. It is a look she has mastered. "Who was that?" she asks.

She probably thinks it's a lover's quarrel. Alison's dying to know about my new man, but I have been vague. I am protective of my privacy.

"Ag, just my mother."

"Really?" She looks surprised. She is not used to me being abrupt with my mother. I usually humour her and let her have her say, no matter what I have going on.

"You wouldn't understand," I say, trying to end our conversation.

"Mothers I do understand!" Alison says in a huff. "You don't have to tell me about mothers . . . but you and your mother seem to get on so well."

I look at Alison, but don't say anything. My mother and I have a polite relationship. Distant, but polite. My colleagues know this. They also know what my mother is like; they have heard the conversations. Still, I try to keep my relationship with my mother to myself. It is better this way, a kind of censoring. I allow only the merest glimpse into my life. Put my best face forward.

Politeness is one of my hallmarks – what Ma, my mother's mother, would have referred to as "having manners".

I am told that I take after my mother. By this, I think that people mean I look like her. I have my mother's dark hair and skin. It is said that I have expressive eyes – laughing eyes – just like hers. My mother is very beautiful. I don't say this because she is my mother. It is a fact. She knows this. Her looks are just another weapon in her arsenal of charm. Like my mother, I have a certain amount of charm, too. My charm is subdued, whereas hers is flagrant, overpowering.

With the help of my manners and charm, I have managed to work my way up to my current position as a copywriter at a respectable advertising agency in Cape Town. I started here almost six years ago, answering the phones. It was the only way I was able to break into the business. In those days, it was all about whom you knew. Affirmative action had barely touched the industry.

Not that I have any complaints. When my friends whinge about their husbands, their jobs, I am understanding – but I seldom offer up my own stories. Strange, how we women are bonded by our suffering. We good-naturedly compete over who has the greatest sorrows: whose man treats her the worst; whose boss is the biggest pain; whose childhood was the most miserable. Over coffee or drinks, we discuss the pills we take to make our lives more bearable. We trade brand names, generics, homeopathic remedies. Our unhappiness becomes a twisted badge of honour.

But unlike my friends, I struggle to recall my past hurts. I don't talk much about my childhood and remember even less. I am grown up now, able to make my own choices. I choose to be content, if not euphoric. There is peace in my life.

No alarms and no surprises

People say that I come from a family of strong women. While it is true about the family of women, I fear that "strong" may be a bit of an overstatement. What is strength, anyway? I think that all of us – everywhere – try to do what we can. Sometimes we are strong in spite of ourselves.

I am a moderate person; I try to avoid extremes. I am never too happy or too sad. I tell myself that small things make me happy. No one is aware of the conscious effort I make to ensure this evenness of mood. I have become a woman of routine. There is comfort in familiarity.

Yet there are days that I struggle to get out of bed. Days when I wake only to pull the blankets over my head so that I almost cannot breathe. There are times that the shrieking wail of the telephone torments me, so that I am unable to answer. Oh, there are a million small things that plague me and keep me awake at night. On really bad days, the sheer emptiness of life hits me in my stomach. Is there such a thing as an unhappiness gene?

I am my mother's child. And in this simple fact lies my biggest fear. My mother is considered beautiful, accomplished; but I know the dark side. All my life, I have learnt to tiptoe around her moods, living in the spaces between which signify calm. My sister and I, who have lived with the craziness and the ups and downs, have developed nice ways of talking about dark, ugly things. Our mother is "having a good day", or she needs someone to "look in on her", or she has been "sounding funny". There is nothing funny about it.

I observe myself vigilantly. Take my emotional temperature at all times. I watch for strains of melancholy; analyse any sadness that descends. For perhaps, if I can catch it at the onset, I can reduce its effects

Much like people who take vitamin C when they feel a cold coming on. And it is not the sadness itself that is frightening; it is that it is all too familiar.

Spark

For the longest time, I had few memories of my childhood. Then suddenly I did. They came at once. Not in slow drips and nuances, but a deluge. Yet I cannot recall the catalyst. There was no tea-soaked madeleine – although perhaps a pumpkin fritter sprinkled with crunchy cinnamon sugar would be more evocative.

Where do I start?

"Always start at the beginning," my mother advised me when I was a young girl, "and the rest will follow."

Spring 1984

I am lying on my back on the front lawn of our house, squinting up at the sky. The sun is fierce and I shield my eyes as I peer up, working out the intricate patterns formed by the clouds. There is another world up there in Heaven and I imagine myself flying, floating.

I love the way the grass feels against my bare legs. Ticklish. The loamy smell of the earth as I turn over and bury my nose is familiar and warm. Then Lili comes outside and sees me.

"Siss, Danny," she pronounces loudly. "Don't you know that dogs pee right where you are lying?"

She torments me as if it is her job. I know what she is trying to do, so I ignore her.

"Mommy," she shouts to our mother inside, "Danika's lying in dog pee!"

Our mother, lost to her pots and pans in the steamy heat of the kitchen, doesn't hear her, or pretends not to. So Lili gives up on trying to upset me and pirouettes round and round the lawn, throwing up her arms, her practised ballerina smile firmly in place. Right now, her biggest concern is that she is growing too tall to be a dancer. We all know that this is the reason why Princess Diana could not become a ballerina.

Lili says that she wants to be a "prima ballerina". I don't know what this means or how it is different from normal ballet dancers, but it sounds pretty and important.

The sun lulls me to sleep. I dream that I am a fairy princess, Nancy Drew and Miss South Africa all rolled into one. I am woken from this reverie by Lili's shrill voice calling me inside as supper is nearly done. Unsteadily, I get up from the lawn, a bit woozy from sleeping in the sun. I note the red grass indents on my skin with some satisfaction, and look around before heading for the front door.

It is quite late now. Neighbourhood men hurriedly walk past our house on their way home from work. Eager for supper, to put their feet up, to take their socks and shoes off, just like my father does when he comes home. He tries to force us to take them off for him, but we refuse because they stink so badly. So badly my mother even buys him the socks with the green stripe for smelly feet. But they do not work, I swear.

All over our neighbourhood, lights go on. Curtains are drawn, hands are washed and prayers are said as families prepare for supper. Rice, potato and meat, bredies, curries, frikkadels. Sometimes the belal sounds while we are eating, calling the Moslems to prayer. This annoys my father. He will glare up from his plate, but usually he will not swear unless they are really loud or we are saying grace. The thing about eating is that you have to be quiet. "And don't leave the table until you've cleared your plate."

Our mother tells us about the starving children in Ethiopia when Lili and I don't want to eat all our food. Those poor children wish they had food to eat, and we are so lucky. So we swallow and chew, chew and swallow, in a rush to finish our supper so that we can watch *The A-Team* on TV – once we've cleaned the kitchen.

I wish that my father would hurry up. My mother has finished eating, but listens attentively as he talks about his day. My father talks very slowly about who said what and what does my mother think? Bored, Lili and I twist around in our chairs and look at the ceiling, at each other, at our father's plate. Eventually, our mother will tell us that we can leave the table and start clearing the plates away, but first we must excuse ourselves properly.

"Excuse me from the table and thank you for the food," we say, like parrots.

My father takes supper time really seriously. And other mealtimes like Sunday lunch. Every Sunday, we have the same things: roast meat or chicken, boiled pumpkin with cinnamon, cauliflower cheese or squash with nutmeg grated on top. Lili and I don't like vegetables, but our father always says, "Waste not, want not." So we force ourselves to eat them. Lili pinches her nose shut when she eats things she doesn't like and I take big gulps. My parents are always telling me to chew my food properly, but I am always in a hurry.

Other things we have to do are: make sure that our elbows do not touch the table, and that we speak only when we are spoken to. But the rules only count when my father is here. When he is away, we eat supper in front of the TV. I ask my mother why we can't always eat like this, but she says it is my father's way. That this is the way he was brought up. Whenever my father does something that we do not like, my mother says it is because of the way he was brought up.

She tells us the story about the first time she had supper at his house. Before they got married. Our father is the eldest of five children and the only boy. He was very spoilt, even though his family was poor, our mother says. Our grandmother, Ma Matthews, dished the stew. First a big plate with most of the meat and potatoes to our grandfather, and then the second-biggest serving to our father. The women, including our mother, shared the rest. "There were only a few bits of meat on the plate," our mother tells us, "and the potatoes were hard because she didn't cook the stew long enough."

Once everyone had gobbled up their food, the younger sisters scrambled for anything left over in the pot – gravy, a bit more rice – but they were quickly elbowed out of the way by my father. I think that is why my mother always dishes such large helpings for him.

Nice families live all around us. We live in a nice neighbourhood. Daddies work, mommies stay at home and children go to school. After school, we do our homework and the Moslem children go to madrasa, another kind of school, which makes me glad that I am not Moslem. Imagine going to school twice in one day!

Next to us lives Tracey. "Racy Tracey" she will be called when she is older, but now she is just Tracey. She is a few months older than I am. We play together after school once our uniforms are hung up and our chores are done. Her family has a big back yard. Her father hasn't been bitten by the renovation bug like mine has, so there is more space for games. When she's naughty, Tracey's mother yells at her, "Wait until Mr English comes home, then you'll get it!" Mr English is her father. I often wonder about that surname, since her parents are actually Afrikaans-speaking, although they talk to her in English. Sometimes I can hear her getting it on the other side of the wall as her father hits her with the grey patent-leather belt that he wears every day except Sundays. On Sundays, he wears a brown belt to match the light brown safari suit he wears to church. Tracey's shrieks make me shudder as I imagine myself on the receiving end of such a punishment. After all, she does not get into trouble all by herself!

Tracey is very impressed by how easy Lili and I have it. Also that we don't have to go to church as often as she does. Not only do they attend the morning and evening services on Sundays, they also attend meetings on Wednesdays, and on Thursdays there's choir practice. Mrs English, whom we call Auntie Ruthie, asks me about this sometimes. "Wouldn't you like to go to church with Tracey?"

I shrug my shoulders and look for an excuse, although *I* am worried when she says that she is worried about what's going to happen to me in the afterlife. My mother always gets very cross when I tell her what Auntie Ruthie says, and calls her a busybody under her breath. We call Mr English Mr English, although his name, Tracey tells me, is Patrick. I think that he is also concerned about me, because he always looks so sad when he sees me. Sometimes he doesn't even greet me back when I call, "Hello Mr English!", loud enough for him to hear me.

Tracey tells me about the farm where the rest of her family still live. They are the only members of their family who live in the city and they visit the farm a lot. One day Tracey returns and tells me about how her uncle ran after a chicken with an axe. When I ask her why he would do such a thing, she looks at me in amazement. "To kill it, of course," she explains, looking at me as if I know nothing. "So we could have it for lunch." Although I sometimes wish that we had family who live upcountry, I'm also glad that we do not.

The days that Tracey plays with Lili, I'm not allowed to join in the game. It is so unfair! Everyone wants to be Lili's friend because she is older and knows so much more than I do. She is so blooming graceful as she practises her ballet steps. I'm another story. How am I ever going to become a prima ballerina like Lili if I can't even do a plié properly? "Not everyone has to be good at ballet," my mother tells me. "You are good at other things."

Although my name is Danika, everyone calls me Danny, except when they are cross with me; then I am Danika. Lili is short for Lilian-Rose, but everyone calls her Lili. My mother is just my mother and my father is just my father. Tracey calls them Mrs and Mr Matthews, although my mother says, "Call me May." My father likes being called Mr Matthews, like Mr English. Maybe that's just how fathers are.

In our back yard there is a huge, spreading mulberry tree. At first Lili was the only one who could climb it, but Tracey and I have found a way. First we grab hold of the lower branches and pull ourselves up, and from there we can reach the higher ones. Soon we can climb all the way to the top. From so high, I can see everywhere: into the neighbours' back yards and far, far away over the rooftops. Maybe even as far as another country.

Before I started school, my father made me a swing out of an old tyre and a length of rope. I love twirling myself round and round, making dust circles in the ground under the mulberry tree until everything spins and I feel dizzy. Lili also likes the swing and is always threatening to tell our mother if I don't let her have a turn. But she is such a show-off, dipping deeper and deeper and kicking her legs higher and higher until she is so high up that I have to get out of the way or I'll get hurt. Her long hair flies wildly behind her back. My father promises to build me a tree house, but he always forgets and when I remind him, he says that his back is sore or he's too tired.

When they are ripe, we eat the purply black mulberries off the tree, still warm from the sun. We don't care that the tart, sweet nectar dribbles down our chins and stains our faces and clothes. If you squash a ripe berry onto your skin and wipe away the tiny seeds, it looks like blood. I enjoy scaring my mother with imaginary hurts. She gets very upset, folding me into her arms, examining my "sore" until I burst out laughing and tell her that I'm only playing.

My mother loves the taste of the mulberries, but she refuses to pick them herself. She hates the thick, hairy caterpillars that overrun the tree. Lili and I are not scared. We torment each other by putting the hairy worms on each other's clothes and sometimes even dropping them down dresses and T-shirts. But only when our mother is not around. She hands us a big cream enamel dish and we pick the berries until our hands are stained maroon with the juice. Then she rinses them and puts them in the fridge for a few hours, and later we eat them, sprinkled with sugar, with slices of vanilla Family Loaf ice cream.

Other times, we make pots of mulberry jam with the mulberries that are too ripe to eat. You have to be careful to watch that the jam doesn't burn and to stir it all the time, even when the spoon becomes too hot to hold, because jam can burn very easily. The heady smell wafts throughout the house, filling the air with its sticky sweetness. Then, once it has cooled, we bottle the jam in empty peanut-butter jars. When the mulberry season is long over, we'll still be enjoying the taste of the berries on hot scones on a Sunday morning. Still licking maroon and purple smears off the sides of our mouths. Using the syrup of the jam as blood for imaginary hurts.

Most of the time my father does not live with us. It's not some story, like when Lili's friend Monique tells us her father works far away at Sasol, although she can't even remember him. My father really does work away, but he comes home for the weekend twice a month. Monique's father never comes home at all. Sometimes I tease her that she doesn't have a father. She deserves it – when she and Lili play together, I'm not allowed to join in their games either. After school they buy lollipops or suckers and slowly lick them in front of me. Lili never buys me one, even when my mother reminds her. When I ask Lili if I can have just one lick, she says, "Yuck, I don't want your germs. Teacher says that's how people get sick."

Monique sniggers at this. My father says Monique is like a peanut gallery: she agrees with everything Lili says and laughs at even her flouest jokes. That is why I tease Monique about her father. I especially like it when I make her cry. Especially because she is older than me. And especially because Lili prefers her to me.

My mother scolds me when she hears about the teasing. Lili tells her, hoping to get me into trouble. My mother makes me say sorry to

Monique and warns me that if she catches me teasing her again, I'll "get it". This is funny, since my mother does not believe in hitting children. Still, something in her calm, slow voice makes me think twice.

I become more covert in my teasing. Now, instead, I ask Monique why she's so dark, or why her hair is so funny. But it's not so funny when my mother hears about it. She tells me that people can't help the way they are born and that everyone is beautiful in God's eyes. Still, I'm glad my hair is long and smooth – sleek, my father calls it. The only problems are the knots and tangles I always have, which my mother attacks with a bottle of Flex conditioner every morning when she brushes my hair. It hurts so much, but I know better than to cry out. It only makes it worse.

My father is a supervisor on the assembly line making cars. I am not sure what an assembly line is, but I think it has something to do with standing together, like when we line up at school for assembly. When I ask my father about this, he tickles me on my chin and tells me that I'm a silly girl.

"Why doesn't Daddy live with us?" It has become important for me to know this, in case Monique or anyone else gets any ideas.

"His job's in Port Elizabeth," my mother explains. "It's too far away for him to drive there every day."

"Then why can't he get a nearer job?"

"All the big car companies are there," my mother says.

"Then why don't we live there, with him?"

"Just because that's how things are."

But it has always been this way, so we don't miss him too much. When he comes home, he brings us biltong and sweets, and lifts me onto his shoulders. It is good to have a father – not like Monique with her make-believe father.

My father thinks I'm the cleverest girl in the whole world. Okay, I don't think that he's very wrong. He calls me his "little doctor" and tells everyone that I will be the first doctor in the family. It doesn't matter that I hate blood and guts; I bask in his attention. I don't tell him that I would rather be a famous detective and solve crimes, like Nancy Drew with her strawberry-blonde hair.

My mother does not work, but then again, most mothers do not work. Monique's mother works in an office in Town, but I think that's because Monique doesn't really have a father, no matter what she says. When my father comes home, my mother is happy and smiles a lot. We have things like steak for supper and my parents share a bottle of wine. Usually, Lili and I are sent to bed early, but we don't really mind. The next morning, our father drops us at school. When I give him a goodbye hug, he slips some money into my hand to spend at the tuck shop later. I am glad about this because our mother usually gives Lili the money to share between the two of us, and I am sure that she cheats me.

It is even better when my father fetches me in the afternoon. As soon as the teacher dismisses the class, I rush outside to where he's waiting. My teacher is very friendly towards him, much friendlier than she is with my mother, and my father smiles at her and picks me up in front of all the other children like I'm a small child, but I don't mind.

Yes, we are all very happy when our daddy is home.

Sunday morning

I am woken by the honking and gabbling of the wild geese that perch on the rooftops of the high buildings in my area. Their chattering sets my nerves on edge, so I pull the duvet up over my head. It is Sunday already and I deserve more sleep after the night I had.

"Shit," I moan aloud when I wake again. The sun is streaming unwelcomely into my bedroom. I don't know how I managed to sleep through the clatter of the geese.

Do I really have to see her today? There are so many other things I could be doing . . . but of course I will. I am nothing if not a dutiful daughter. I may complain about it, but I always do the right thing as far as my mother is concerned.

When she hears noises in the middle of the night and is convinced that someone is trying to break in, she calls me; she knows that I will drive through to check it out, no matter what the time. I am the one in whom she confides, to whom she tells her fears and little secrets. Nothing is too personal or too intimate. My role is that of a listener. The background. She is the central figure.

I rush through my cup of coffee. It is best to get this over with. I still need to do my washing.

Outside the house, Lady barks in recognition and comes up to me, wagging her tail. Ignoring the dog, I let myself into the house with my key. Louis Armstrong is blaring his saxophone and singing "What a Wonderful World". The music is so loud, my mother does not hear me come in. Her back is to the door as she washes the dishes. Her mind is somewhere outside the kitchen window.

"Why don't you turn the sound down? You can't hear yourself think in that racket!"

My mother turns around, startled.

"What's for lunch?" I ask, sniffing the air expectantly for the familiar Sunday smell of her roast chicken, made with too much garlic.

Drying her hands on a clean drying-up cloth, she looks at me and smiles, "Hello to you too." She is far too cheerful. Without waiting for a reply, she barrels on: "I didn't make anything. I thought we could go out for lunch!"

I look at her, surprised. This is quite unlike her. "Okay," I agree, "but we'll take my car."

I am happy to go. I find this house oppressive and sad, like the cloying scent of potpourri that pervades the air.

We drive in silence. Eventually, my mother fiddles with the radio and finds the station that plays the jazz. I say nothing, although I am not too fond of that kind of music.

"Where shall we go?" I ask.

"What do you feel like?"

So I drive to the beach. A regular Sunday thing. When we were younger, my mother would sometimes take Lili and me to Hout Bay for fish and chips when my father was not around. The two of us would sit on the back seat, sharing our parcel and comparing portion sizes to see who got the most chips or the biggest piece of fish. Lazy Sundays. My mother would park at the beach and we would watch the waves as we ate. Then Lili and I would chase the seagulls while my mother read the *Sunday Times*.

I do not like eating in my car since it is still quite new, so we go to a seafood restaurant near the beach instead.

The bombshell

This isn't so bad after all, I think as I stare out across the ocean while the sun casts its shimmer over the calm, still water.

"So, Mom," I say, taking a sip of my icy Chardonnay, "what's new?"

"I'm dying," my mother announces.

My wine goes down the wrong way as I choke on her words. "Dying?" I echo, not sure of what I've heard.

"I've been to the doctors – more than one – and they all agree."

"What do you mean?" I ask. "Why didn't you tell me sooner?"

This was not part of the deal. All I came for was lunch.

My mother says, "Let me start at the beginning . . ."

Spring 1984

On the Sundays that my father is away, we go to Ma's house for lunch. We go early so that my mother can read her *Sunday Times* at the kitchen table. Lili and I help Ma as she prepares the lunch – peeling, mixing, washing the dishes.

I like it when Ma lets me knead the dough for bread. We know that Ma gets up early on Sunday mornings to start the bread so that it can be done in time. "Bread takes a long time to make," she tells us, "and you know, the shops don't make bread on a Sunday. First the yeast has to prove, then the dough has to rise and then you punch it out and it has to rise again." Ma's bread is her pride and joy. "In the old days, people had to make their own bread," she explains. "My mother couldn't afford to buy a loaf of bread every day. Not with nine mouths to feed!" Ma loves to talk about the old days and how hard she had it when she was growing up.

"What did you eat on the bread, Ma?" I ask, although I already know the answer.

Ma dusts the flour off her apron and smiles as if she sees her dead mother's kitchen in front of her. "My family was so poor," Ma says, "that all we had to eat on our bread was fat."

"What's that again, Ma?" Lili asks. She hates it when I get all the attention.

"My mother used to buy tail fat from the butcher and melt it down slowly on the stove. She'd stir it and stir it until it was smooth. Then she'd put it in a bakkie and keep it in the cooler."

"Why didn't she put it in the fridge then?" I ask.

Lili interrupts, "But how did it taste? Imagine eating fat. Yuck-key!"

"Oh, it was the most delicious thing you could ever taste," Ma insists. "It tasted just like meat, and there were little pieces of meat in the spread. And of course you know that we didn't have things like fridges back then!"

Lili looks at me as if to say Ma is mad. Ma furiously punches the dough back. Then she shapes it into loaves and puts them in the greased loaf tins to rise in the warmer oven. I have my own piece of dough that I make into shapes. Ma lets me put them in the oven when the bread is nearly done. That is the best part of making bread.

On Mondays we take the home-made bread to school with leftover meat and beetroot salad – the whole sandwich is pink from the beetroot. But Ma's bread is not soft like the shop's bread. It is hard and it hurts your mouth when you chew. It's not neatly sliced like shop bread either. My mother cuts the bread into thick slices. Some children come to school with rolls, but my mother won't buy them on a Sunday. Not when we have all that bread!

Ma never comes to our house for lunch. When I ask her about it, she laughs and says it's because my mother can't cook to save her life, but I don't think this is true since my mother makes very nice food.

When my father is home, we go to church on a Sunday. We have to wake up early to be ready in time. Church is really long, more than three hours. Afterwards, my father greets everyone and shakes the men's hands and kisses the women on their cheeks and tells them how lovely they're looking. I have to greet everyone too and smile, even if the ladies pinch my cheeks and tell me it's nice to see us in church again. Still, it's not as bad as Tracey has it.

After church, we go straight to my father's family. When Lili and I nag to rather go to Ma's house for lunch, our father tells us that we see enough of that Ma when he's away and we should visit our other Ma. But I don't like Ma Matthews's food, and everyone talks too loudly, and I feel like I'm being squashed in the cramped-up lounge. When it's too hot or crowded, my mother lets me and Lili play outside, as long as one of my father's sisters watches us. We're not allowed to go outside the gate. Not even on the pavement. It is dangerous here, my mother warns, and we must not talk to strangers. Erica, my youngest aunt – she's the one who is usually told to look after us – comes outside, then she goes to stand with the boys and girls on the corner. They talk loudly in Afrikaans and look at me and Lili from time to time and laugh. Lili and I laugh at the girls because they think it's okay to walk around with stockings on their hair or with big orange and green rollers. Even Erica walks around like that. "But what can you expect?" Lili says.

♠

Our mother is going to have a baby. I am very happy when she tells me and Lili the news. Some of the girls in my class who have baby brothers and sisters like to brag about them. Plus, I am tired of being the baby. I can't wait to be a big sister. *My* big sister is not as impressed.

"As if one wasn't enough," she says. And, "At your age!"

But in fact, our parents are young. Younger than the other mothers and fathers. It is a secret that our parents had to get married. Our mother says that it is no one's business. That's what she said the day Lili came home from school and told her that her teacher had remarked – in front of the whole class – that our mother was very young to be the mother of such a big girl.

Our mother fell pregnant with Lili when she was sixteen years old and still in high school. The way she talks about school, with a half-smile on her face, you'd think that her life was a kind of fairy-tale life before this happened. She was so clever, she says with a faraway look on her face.

"Were you the cleverest girl in the class, then?" I ask, but I know the answer already. We've heard the story many times before.

"Mm," our mother replies, "and all the nuns loved me. They used to plait my hair during break."

"Was your hair really long, then?" I ask, shaking my plaits just a little.

"Down to my bum. Long and black, just like yours, Danny."

Then, before I can even ask another question, she continues. "The nuns had so many plans for me, you know. I was going to go to university. Maybe become a doctor. Or a lawyer."

The only way that Ma would allow her to keep the baby was if she got married. Not that she has any regrets, she's quick to tell Lili, who frowns whenever the story is told.

And that is the story of my family.

I am so excited about the new baby that I tell everyone. Even though it's supposed to be a secret. I tell my teachers and my friends at school. I tell Tracey from next door, making her toss in to keep the secret. I even tell Ma.

"Well, it's her own life," Ma says out loud, but not really to me. "What does that woman think she's doing? If she wants to ruin her life, I wash my hands of her."

When I get home, I ask my mother what it means to wash your hands of someone. Do you just have to wash your hands a lot? "Where did you hear that?" my mother asks. "Is your grandmother filling your head with rubbish again?" she demands. Her face goes very red and I can tell that she is cross. "Go and play outside," she tells me and Lili.

Lili gives me a look as if to say, "What did you do now?"

My mother is furiously punching in numbers on the telephone as we slip out the back door, careful not to bang it.

When I come back inside, I've forgotten about my mother's anger. It is only after a few weeks that I realise we no longer visit Ma like we used to do. When I ask my mother about this, she says that it's not true, that I'm imagining things and she's just been busy. Later, Lili says that it's my fault that Ma and my mother are not speaking. Ever since I told our mother what Ma said about the new baby. Lili says that she knows better than to tell people things that will only hurt their feelings.

The person who is the most excited about the new baby is my father. He tells everyone about it. He is convinced that this baby is going to be a boy. He talks about all the things he is going to teach this son of his. How to swim. How to fish. I think to myself that these sound like fun things to do, but I say nothing. He's never offered to teach me or Lili how to swim or how to fish.

He is so excited about the baby that he phones every day when he's away to check up on my mother and to hear if we are helping her. Ma Matthews also comes to visit us, even though she has to take a train and a bus to get here from Retreat.

We are very surprised by her visits – she never used to visit us when my father wasn't there. My mother gets very cross when she comes over. Ma Matthews says things under her breath about "my son" all the time. Like, "Why is my son's house so dirty?" My mother says she acts like it's her duty to keep the house spotless. She comes once a week now – to clean. First, while she sits on the couch and takes her shoes off, she tells Lili to make her a cup of tea. Then, once the tea is drunk up, she takes her apron out of the plastic Shoprite packet she always carries it in. She's now ready for cleaning, walking around the house in her beige pantyhose. Lili and I are very glad that it's time for school, or else she'd force us to help her.

When I get home from school, she is still cleaning. As she works, she offers my mother advice on how to keep a house. "You are so lucky," she tells her, "my son really spoils you." She is so old, but she goes down on her hands and knees to scrub the floors, not caring about messing up her pantyhose.

Our mother says to us, "I draw the line at that woman cooking for us." This is after Ma Matthews has offered to teach her to make all my father's favourite foods. "Do you know that she puts sugar and cloves in all her food?"

We smile broadly. We love it when she complains to us about Ma Matthews.

But to Ma Matthews she just says sweetly, "No, thank you. Trevor likes my food."

Ma Matthews looks so hurt that I almost feel sorry for her – but then I remember how she's always complaining about how lazy Lili and I are. And how spoilt. Like two little misses. She cannot believe it when Lili says she can't help clean because she has homework, and I explain how I can't dust or polish because of my allergies.

"You're spoiling those girls, May," she says. "Now *my* girls know how to clean!"

My mother just shrugs and smiles. "Ag, they're still young, and they've got school," she explains.

"But that's no excuse," Ma Matthews continues. "I must have a word with Trevor. What good will these girls be once they're older?"

When she goes home, the three of us make fun about how much she loves to clean.

My mother is never without her knitting bag now. Delicate bootees and matinée jackets slip off her knitting needles in pale yellow, lime and pure white. I'm not allowed to touch her knitting. Not since I picked up a shawl she was busy with and tried to follow the pattern, and ended up dropping the stitches off the needle. Not even to gently move it off her lap or detangle it from her hands when she falls asleep where she's sitting, like she always does. Ma Matthews scolds her and tells her that pregnant women aren't supposed to knit. That the wool goes around the baby's neck and strangles it. My mother pulls a face behind her back and ignores her.

"Can the wool really strangle the baby?" I ask my mother when Ma Matthews isn't around.

"Of course not!" my mother says with a loud, brittle laugh. "It's just another old wives' tale."

"What's an old wives' tale?" I ask, but she must not have heard me, because she doesn't answer.

♠

We nag and nag our mother to take us to visit Ma.

"But why can't we visit Ma?" I keep asking, until Lili gives me a look to keep quiet.

"Your Ma is just being unreasonable," our mother says with a scowl. "But if you girls really want to see her, I can't stop you. You girls must phone her and make your own arrangements."

Lili smiles broadly, as if it's all thanks to her that our mother has given in. She phones Ma to ask her when we can come visit.

We have so much to say to Ma when we visit her on Saturday. She is so happy to see us that she gives us both a big hug. Later, we sit in the kitchen and tell her all about Ma Matthews. We know she will laugh, like she used to do with our mother when the two of them talked about our other Ma.

She listens to our stories, but this time she does not laugh. She just shakes her head and says, "Well, what can you expect of those people?"

We look at her, but she doesn't say anything more. Instead, she grabs her gardening hat and says, "Come, girls, come help me in the garden."

We love playing in Ma's big garden and listening to her stories so much that we almost don't want to leave when it is time for her to take us home. But it's nearly time for supper and our mother is expecting us, Ma says.

On the way home, I play Volksie with myself, because Lili doesn't like to play the game with me any more. Plus she cheats. Ma and Lili keep quiet until Lili says softly, "Ma, how come you don't like my daddy?"

Squinting against the fading sun, Ma lifts her eyes from the road. "Don't be silly. What gave you that idea? I have nothing against your father!"

♠

My father comes home all the time now that my mother is pregnant. He still brings us biltong and still lifts me in the air, but he doesn't play with me as much as he used to. He also does not fetch me from school any more.

When he is home, he talks about "his son" all the time. Just like Ma Matthews talks about her "grandson". Both of them are sure that my mother is going to have a baby boy. A son is important, they say, so that he can carry on the family name. I ask, "What about me, why can't I carry on the family name?" But it's not the same, they insist.

Ma Matthews is a troublemaker, my mother says. She's the one who tells my father how lazy Lili and I are. She says to him, "They are such little madams," and I know that this is a bad thing. There is nothing worse that being too big for your boots.

"You girls must help your mother more!" our father shouts at us when he comes back from dropping Ma Matthews at home. I'm not used to my father shouting at me, so I run to my bedroom in tears.

My mother is angry too. The next morning, she furiously brushes my hair until I cry out in pain. She looks at me in amazement when I tell her that she is hurting me.

"Are you also cross with me?" I ask.

She bends down and hugs me, even though it's difficult for her with her big stomach in the way. "You're my girl," she says, smiling. "I love you just the way you are."

This time, I am not so sad when my father leaves.

Try not to breathe

The flow is relentless. Now that she has chosen to open up, my mother cannot stop.

"How long have you known?" I ask.

"Not long."

I stare out the window at the view I was admiring a moment ago. Tears prickle at the corners of my eyes, but I don't give in to them. I take a deep breath. I know that I have to be strong now.

"Does Lili know?"

"No. Not yet."

"We'll be okay," I venture, to fill the space.

I do not ask her the one question burning within me. *How long?*

As if divining my thoughts, my mother says, "The doctors can't say how long."

"Can I meet with your doctors then?" I ask. It is a statement, not a question.

"I have an appointment for tomorrow," she replies, no doubt hoping that this is too short notice for me to rearrange my diary.

"I'll come with you, Mom," I offer. "I'll just go in to work later," I say, mentally juggling my schedule.

"You don't have to do it, Danny," my mother demurs, but I will not take no for an answer. I can be stubborn too.

She relents. "Can we try to get there early then?"

"Of course," I reply. "I'll fetch you."

Just sitting here waiting

But of course I take my time. I savour my morning coffee – after all, there is no rush. We'll get there when we get there, I reason. Anyway, my mother is never ready on time.

She is sitting just inside the open front door when I pull up outside her house. She doesn't wait for me to come in; she starts to lock the door and walks towards the car.

"Where were you?" she asks lightly, but I can tell from the set of her face that she is not happy that I am late.

"It's still early," I say. "We have plenty of time."

"We'll see," my mother says primly, but says no more.

She is right; we are late. Already there is a long queue of people settled in for the wait. First we have to place her hospital card in the correct pile and take a number from a box, then we have to queue for her folder. After this, we have to wait for someone else to glance at the folder and redirect us to another queue. Then we can see the doctor.

"We should have come earlier. We would have had the folder by now," my mother volunteers.

I say nothing.

I am learning.

The wooden bench we have to sit on is filthy. Am I really expected to sit here? I tell my mother to sit, that I will stand; but eventually my feet tire in their high heels and I succumb. Grimy initials are carved all along the seat and back rest. Probably written on the walls too, although I can see that they have been painted recently, a seasick colour between khaki and grey. The hospital smell of antiseptic and decay pervades the air. I sniff my wrists obsessively, even though I am wearing my least favourite perfume today. A well-meant gift from a man who did not know me very well. My mother does not seem to notice the stench. Maybe she is used to it, I muse, or maybe her sickness has affected her olfactory glands.

Three hours later and I am fuming at the outrage. "Look at the time! How long have we been sitting on this same bench?" I do not care whom I offend. A shackled prisoner walks by in his bright orange jump suit with the word "prisoner" stamped all over it. His warder is right behind him, but it is scant consolation. Please don't sit next to me, I silently intone; I do not make eye contact. My gaze is fixed intently on his leg irons, as if to reassure myself that he cannot escape. My prayer is answered and they move on.

Occasionally, a stranger smiles weakly and hesitantly at me, but I refuse to respond. I have not come here for conversation. I need to get back to work and I need to pee. There is no way that I can use the toilets here. How much longer?

Eventually my mother's name is called.

"Should I go in with you?" I ask.

"No, I'm fine," she replies. "I'll try to hurry up," she adds as an after-thought.

"Take your time," I say politely, but I do not mean it.

While my mother is in with the doctor, I pace up and down the corridor, fielding calls from my office. "Still here," I say, trying to sound bright and in control. "I'll come as soon as I can."

The wait is interminable. Resigned, I have given up looking at my watch. When my mother finally comes out, I ask her what took so long.

"There were student doctors . . . my doctor was explaining things to them."

I had forgotten that Groote Schuur was a teaching hospital. How can my mother handle a bunch of strangers gawking at her like that?

Snake oil

By the time I find out about my mother's disease, it is too late to do anything about it. Too late for dietary and lifestyle changes. Too late for spirulina and other "miracle" cures. But still I search. I trawl the Internet for information. The only thing I learn is that with this disease, death is inevitable. I meet with my mother's doctors and they tell me the same thing.

She insists on attending the state hospital, even though Lili and I offer to help her. "They have the best facilities for this," my mother informs me.

It doesn't make me feel better.

"At least go and see a specialist in private practice," I say firmly.

But he tells us the same thing. The disease is too far advanced to be cured. All we can do is manage it. And hope for the best. I don't know what this means.

"Didn't you feel it coming?" I ask my mother, aghast. "Surely you knew that you were not well?"

But it is too late for recrimination, for "Why didn't they find it sooner?" Time is running out. Armed with the knowledge of her disease, I am practical, almost calm. I know what signs to look for.

My mother is still young – only forty-eight. This is not the way it was meant to be. Not like this.

Summer 1984/85

I am so excited when I get my first report card, I can't wait to get home. My mother opens it and says she always knew I was clever. This is just the proof. I imagine how happy my father will be when he sees it. Lili scowls and says that everyone gets a good report in Sub A, but she is just being Lili. My mother is cross with her because she did badly at maths. Lili says smartly, "What's the use of maths? Ballerinas don't need maths."

My mother tells her that she's wrong; that we use maths every day. Grown-ups too. "How will you know if you get the right change when you go to the shop?" she asks.

I make the mistake of reciting Lili's times tables that she practised in front of the mirror in our room every night before her exam. Except I don't fumble over the numbers, they come easily to me. I get them all right. Right up to the six times table, which is as far as Lili's class went. My mother looks at me in amazement. "Why can't you be more like your little sister?" she says. Lili glares at me, lifts onto her toes in one of her ballet poses and glides out of the room.

I am so used to going to school that I'm soon bored with the holidays. Whenever it's even a little hot, the three of us go the beach. Most people go to Strandfontein, which is nearer, but we go to the Camps Bay tidal pool, which my mother says is much cleaner. Also, there's not that many "funny" people on the beach. My mother says that's because people have to pay to get in, so it keeps "the element" out. Although I don't know what this means, I nod my head.

I love floating on my back in the water. My mother never swims. She rolls up her pants and stands at the edge of the water, watching us swim. Eventually Lili and I tire and we lie on our towels on the lawn, picking at the cold chicken and boiled eggs that our mother packed in, while the sun warms our salt-licked bodies. I stand up and flick my long, wet hair. If our mother is in a good mood, we go to Sea Point for ice cream, three scoops, which we eat in the car before we drive home. Sometimes we're so tired by the time we get home that we fall asleep on top of our beds, still wearing our bathers.

We went to Strandfontein once, with my father's friends. But that beach was really crowded. Another time we went to Kalk Bay beach with Ma, but the sand was brownish and we had to walk through a tunnel to get to the beach. It smelled like pee in the tunnel and Lili and I complained all the time, until Ma crossly said it was time for us to go home.

Ma Matthews doesn't believe we should go to the beach. Any beach. She says to my mother that she mustn't let us spend so much time in the sun because it'll make us dark. My mother tells her that she doesn't have a problem with us being dark. I don't understand why Ma Matthews cares about whether we're dark or not. When I ask my mother, all she says is that Ma Matthews is a stupid woman.

As summer continues, my mother starts to say she's too tired to take us to the beach. Lili and I know it helps to work together, so we complain about how hot it is all the time. Eventually, my mother comes up with a plan. She puts the sprinkler on the lawn and we put on our bathers and run through it, taking turns to see who can stay in the middle the longest.

But Lili thinks that she is the boss of the sprinkler. She invites Monique to come and play by her and there is even less time for me in the sprinkler. Still, I know one way to make Monique go home – tease her about her father. "Do you really have a daddy?" I ask for the millionth time. "How come we never see him?"

This trick still makes Monique cry like a big baby. When Lili tells our mother about it, she gets so cross that I am not allowed to play in the sprinkler for a whole day. I am so bored.

Christmas is around the corner and soon my father will be home. I can't wait to see what he'll bring me. My mother is no fun now that the baby is coming. We never do fun things and she is always resting. Even in this heat.

For once, Lili and I are friends. Monique does not come around any more, but Lili doesn't mind too much. Monique is foolish, she says, and cries too much. So we play together. I think Lili is only being nice so that she can get good presents, but I don't mind. I also want good presents, so we are both behaving ourselves.

Ma comes to fetch us to help her get ready for Christmas, like she does every year. Lili writes out her Christmas cards in her neatest handwriting while Ma dictates lengthy messages, pausing occasionally to spell out difficult words. When that's done, Lili helps her to wrap presents for Auntie Astrid and her family and then package them in a brown cardboard box, along with bottles of jam and konfyt. Auntie Astrid is our mother's only sister. I am fascinated by her.

"Ma, how come Auntie Astrid moved to Canada?" I want to know. This question has bothered me for so long. I also want to know why my mother refuses to talk to Auntie Astrid, but I dare not ask Ma. Not with her and my mother already not speaking to each other.

We have never met Astrid – she left the country long before Lili and I were born. Still, Ma keeps the memory of her eldest daughter fresh. She's so proud of her, this beautiful woman with the fair complexion and the sparkling green eyes. Another thing in Auntie Astrid's favour is that she married an Italian. A Canadian, but an Italian nevertheless.

"Yes my girl, a real Italian – speaks Italian and all!" My mother refers to Auntie Astrid as "that foolish woman". But I don't tell Ma this.

Sometimes Auntie Astrid sends clothes that her children have out-grown, and my mother sniffs and says, "Who does she think she is? Does she think my children only deserve her children's cast-offs?"

We give the clothes to the poor.

We only know Auntie Astrid and her family through the photo-graphs Ma so proudly displays on her dressing table, and the strange old clothes. Ricardo is two years younger than Lili and Alana is a year younger than me.

Alana is very pretty, like a doll with her pink cheeks and button nose. Ma says she looks very European. I feel so ugly when I compare the two of us. Why can't I be pretty like a princess in the stories? I look at my dark skin and the thick eyebrows that stretch across my face, and I know that I will never be a beauty like my mother or my aunt. Nor pretty like my sister or my cousin. I ask Ma why she doesn't keep a photograph of me next to her bed. Is it because I'm not so pretty?

"Of course not!" she replies. "It's just because Alana is so far away and you girls are right here."

I give Ma a look to tell her that I'm not buying it.

It doesn't help that I know Lili is her favourite. I think it's because she was born first, but when I ask, Ma says I must stop being silly and that grandmothers have no favourites. I point out that it is Lili who always gets to spend weekends with her. Ma says that I must forget my nonsense, we must start on the Christmas puddings since they take almost all day.

"Go wash your hands first, Danny," she reminds me, as if I don't already know that you're supposed to wash your hands before you cook.

As I help Ma with the Christmas puddings, which she steams in a big pot on the stove, I forget my displeasure. I help her measure out the flour, the mixed fruit, the raisins and the nuts in empty yoghurt cups. Ma lets me throw in the exotic-smelling spices teaspoonful by teaspoonful. I crack the eggs on the side of the big enamel dish before I plop them into the middle, careful not to get any shell into the mixture.

Then Ma pours in the brandy and the pudding takes on a different smell. All through the year, Ma hoards silver five-cent pieces, which we boil before adding them to the pudding. Although it is my job to help with the pudding, I relinquish the sticky wooden spoon to Lili for a little while so that she can stir the fruity mix and make a wish. We take turns to make our wishes on the Christmas puddings. When we ask Ma what she wished for, she replies with a heavy sigh, "I wish for happiness for all my children."

We look at her, hurt.

"And my grandchildren, of course."

♠

Spurred on by the Christmas puddings, Lili decides that this year we will make home-made presents for the adults. The *Argus* had an article on how to make home-made presents, and Lili tore out the page with recipes for peppermint creams, fudge and coconut ice. We ask my mother if we can go to Shoprite to buy presents and, surprisingly, she agrees.

Shoprite is quite a long way from where we live. We have to cross Lansdowne Bridge to get there – and always by the pedestrian crossing, my mother warns. I walk slowly, admiring some people's gardens and staring at strangers in the road. But Lili is no-nonsense: we have a job to do, "So stop being a baby and just walk!" She can be so mean sometimes . . . but I hurry up, because what will happen to me if she walks away? I know how dangerous Lansdowne Road is.

We buy the coconut and the other ingredients with our change. I can't believe my eyes when Lili buys us each a Surfjoy sucker. The sucker melts and drips orange-red all over my pretty top and even on my hair. But I don't care. I am so happy walking in the road with my big sister that I don't mind when she shakes her head at me and calls me a slob.

I have to change my clothes and wash my hands before Lili allows me to help her make the sweets. All I am allowed to do is stir the pots once she has given them a good stir herself. Then I have to grease the tins. I watch Lili as she carefully pours the fudge into one tin. Then it's time to do the coconut ice. She puts half the mixture into an oiled tin and the other half she carefully colours with cochineal. "Just a drop," she explains.

She puts the pink mixture on top of the white mixture and generously offers me the bowl to lick out. I sit at the table, eating out the dish, and watch as she drops spoonfuls of peppermint cream onto the baking sheet.

"Now all we have to do is wait for it to set," Lili tells me. "Danny, you're in charge of seeing that Mommy doesn't come into the kitchen for at least three hours."

I don't know how I am going to do this, but I'm too busy wiping the bowls clean with my fingers to disagree.

The coconut ice is delicious. First Lili cuts it into squares – I'm too small to use the sharp knife. Then she passes it to me to put it in the small packets. We look and look for a place to hide it where our mother can't find it – until Lili suggests under our beds. It is too difficult for our mother to bend down, so we hide everything there.

We get the peppermint drops out of the fridge. They haven't set very well, but they'll do, so we add them to the packets under the bed. The fudge is not so successful, it doesn't set at all, so we take it to my mother and the three of us take turns digging out the rich goo with spoons. We tell her that we only made fudge.

A few days later, we discover a long trail of ants marching across our bedroom wall.

"Damn it all!" Lili shouts. "The ants have eaten all our sweets!"

All that remains of our hard work is a sticky syrup covered in dead ants. We have to buy presents after all.

"Do I have to buy presents for my daddy's family?" I ask my mother. They never give us presents. At all.

"Of course you do," my mother says.

Even Lili is upset about this. We decide to club our money and buy them a set of glasses. "They never have enough glasses at their house," our mother says.

When my father comes home, he tells us that my mother shouldn't cook and that we will be having Christmas lunch at his parents' house this year. We can't believe this, but we say nothing, because we don't want to make trouble when presents are involved. My mother also says nothing. She stretches her lips very wide as if she is smiling, but I know that she isn't really.

♠

Christmas is my favourite thing in the world. On Christmas Eve, Lili and I go with our father to find the biggest tree. This year, the tree is so big that the top part bends over against the ceiling. Lili and I help our father decorate the tree, but our mother says she has a headache and has to lie down. No one else has a real tree. Not Ma and not Tracey. Their trees come in a box and you have to bend the branches straight before you can hang the trimmings on them. My father's family doesn't believe in Christmas trees. Lili says that it makes sense, since they have no place to put one. We try to stay awake to open our presents exactly at twelve o'clock, but at ten o'clock our father sends us to bed. We have to wake up early for church.

I get the most beautiful doll with long red hair from my parents. My father says the presents are from Father Christmas, but I know there is no such thing. Lili is happy with the roller skates left at the bottom of the tree and the Tinkerbell lipstick my mother helped me choose for her. She gives me a lot of yellow and red and blue bangles and I put them all on my arm.

"Do we have to go to church?" Lili asks hopefully as she straps on her skates.

"Come, get done, girls," our father says. There is no way we will ever miss church at Christmas time.

But for once, Lili and I don't mind sitting three hours in church. The only person who seems cross is our mother. She has been in a bad mood all morning. Shouting at me and Lili to pick up the wrapping paper we left lying on the floor as we tore open our presents. Maybe it's the baby that's bothering her. Her stomach is so swollen now; it looks like she swallowed a watermelon whole. It is so hard – it feels like a watermelon too.

We don't have much time to play with our new toys after church before it is time to go to lunch. "Why can't we rather eat here?" I ask when my mother tells me to leave my new doll at home.

"Why don't you ask your father?" my mother says as we walk to the car, where he is already waiting.

We smile nicely at everyone and wish everyone Merry Christmas, pretending not to mind when Ma Matthews reaches over to kiss us on our lips. But we don't enjoy the lunch. First of all, there aren't enough crackers for everyone, so we have to share. My mother pulls with me and lets me keep the whistle that pops out. My father pulls with Lili, but he likes the key ring so much he decides to keep it for himself. What does Lili need a key ring for in any case, he reminds her.

It is true that Ma Matthews doesn't cook like us. There's a big turkey on the table, but it is not cooked properly inside and I hate to eat bloody food. The peas and carrots are watery and soft, and there's even a dish of haddock-and-pea macaroni on the table among the other dishes. Who eats macaroni at Christmas? The gravy for the turkey is sweet. Must be from all the sugar Ma Matthews adds to her food, I think.

Then it's time for pudding. My aunts bring out bowls of jelly and custard and peaches – but where is the trifle? Where is the Christmas pudding that we always have? I don't like the way Christmas pudding tastes, but it has real five-cent pieces in it and if you find one, you can make a wish and your wish will come true.

After lunch, our father tells me and Lili to go help in the kitchen. I look at him in surprise, silently begging him not to force us to clean on Christmas Day, but he narrows his eyes and gives me a look that says he's serious. It is so unfair!

We run the tap, waiting for the water to heat up. After a long, long time, the water still isn't hot. "Maybe it will only get hot much later . . ." Lili whispers to me.

"Like when we get home, you mean?" I ask.

"Exactly!" Lili says, grinning broadly.

We go back into the lounge and Lili tells our father that there is no hot water.

Ma Matthews looks at us, her eyes narrowing as she frowns. "What do you think we are, fancy like yous? Don't you know that we don't have hot water in this house? We have to boil all the hot water we use in this house."

She motions to Erica, the youngest sister. "Erica, go show the madams how to use the urn. You'd better watch them." By this time, the brandy and Coke has come out and the lit cigarettes are creating a haze in the stuffy room. Our eyes burn with hatred and resentment, but the mood in the tiny flat is so rancorous and alive, we say nothing, rather than provide a spark for all the suppressed emotions.

"No wonder she likes to come to our house all the time," I whisper to Lili, loud enough for Erica to hear.

As we leave, Ma Matthews says loudly as she takes a sip from her drink, "It's so nice to see the young madams help for a change."

Bravely and treacherously, Lili responds in her best English accent: "Yes it is!"

My mother puts her hand on Lili's shoulder and we walk out. No one speaks during the ride home. I can't wait for my mother to have this baby so that things can go back to normal.

♠

We don't see Ma before Christmas lunch and when Lili calls her, the phone just rings and rings. I feel sad and wonder who she is spending the day with. We know how much Ma loves Christmas. I think about horrible old Ma Matthews and miss Ma even more.

There is one thing that we can always rely on Ma for and that is good presents. Sometimes Auntie Astrid's presents reach Ma's house in time for Christmas. She always sends presents for Lili and me. Lovely Canadian chocolates and toys.

When we come back home from the awful lunch, my father promises to take us to Ma once he's had a nap. Eating makes my father very tired, so he always has a nap after lunch. My mother is always tired these days, so she also sleeps. My mother's stomach is so big that it can't fit behind the steering wheel of the car; that is why my father has to take us.

When we finally go to wish Ma, it's already starting to get dark. My father doesn't come into Ma's house. Nor does he wish her. He stays in the car, his fingertips tapping a restless beat on the steering wheel.

The lights of her tree are on and twinkling and underneath it are several beautifully wrapped presents. Auntie Astrid's presents made it in time! Along with the presents for me and Lili is a present for the baby. Ma is so happy to see the two of us that her eyes twinkle and shine, just like the lights on the tree. She hugs us and wishes us a merry Christmas.

"Look at how well the puddings came," she exclaims, walking us to the kitchen. "Don't forget to take one home for your mother!"

We sit at the kitchen table eating our favourite trifle and Lili tells her about how terrible the lunch was.

"And they forced us to clean," I chime in, knowing that Ma will take my part.

"Ag, what can you do?" my grandmother sighs, as my father hoots impatiently from the car. "The problem is, those people are not like us."

This time I know better than to tell anyone what Ma said.

Soon it is New Year's Eve and our parents give me and Lili permission to spend the night at Ma's house, like we do every year. Once more, our father drops us off and once more he does not come in. He hoots loudly as he goes.

Ma makes us sandwiches with the leftover Christmas meat and beet-root salad on thick slices of home-made bread. My mouth waters as I watch her make these ungainly sandwiches. How I have missed them.

Later, once the crumbs have been brushed off and we have bathed and brushed our teeth, we settle down to watch TV with Ma. Every year she tells us that it's important to face the new year clean, but I don't know why.

Lili pours Ma a rum and Coke and very carefully slices the lemon. I'm not allowed to use such sharp knives. Ma takes a sip and pronounces the drink perfect – just the right combination of rum, Coke, ice and lemon. Lili glows in her praise. Even though I am very sleepy, I will myself to stay awake. Then, as midnight nears, Ma opens a small bottle of sparkling wine and pours a tiny bit into champagne glasses for all three of us. When it is exactly twelve o' clock, the three of us toast one another and make our wishes for the new year.

A short while after midnight, we hear the approaching drums that herald the arrival of the coons as they march to the old-age home opposite Ma's house to perform for the old people. This is a New Year's Eve tradition, Ma says. It is part of the reason why we love to spend New Year's Eve at Ma's house. The wily performers in their colourful costumes hopping, dancing and singing their ghoema music enthral me. With their Nugget-smeared faces and sinister smiles, they horrify me too.

We rush outside and stand on the stoep. All the neighbours are standing on their stoeps. We call across, wishing one another Happy New Year. For that moment, the world is at peace. All petty arguments, like who doesn't pick up the rubbish in front of his house, or whose dog barks all night, keeping the rest of the neighbourhood awake, are forgotten.

We sleep late on New Year's day and are woken by my father's insistent hooting outside. It's time to go back home.

My mother asks us if the coons came and we tell her all about it, but then she is tired and we have to leave her alone so that she can rest.

Before long, my father has to go back to work. As he leaves, he tells me and Lili to be good, and that he's sure the next time he sees us, we'll have a baby brother.

"Or sister," Lili says, but he says no, he is sure it will be a boy.

"Do you want another sister then?" I ask Lili.

"I cannot stand boys," she replies haughtily.

Beautiful girl

I am running late for work when she calls.

"Danny," my mother says tremulously.

"What's wrong, Mom?" I ask. "Is everything okay?"

"I need a favour," she says, "but you can tell me if you don't want to do it."

"What is it, Mom?" I say curtly. I am late after all.

"I need a lift," she says vaguely.

"To hospital?"

"No . . . yes."

"What is it, Mom?" I repeat. "I'm going to be late for work."

"Oh, if it's a problem, just tell me."

"I never said it was a problem, Mom. Tell me what you want."

"I have an appointment at the salon later on this afternoon. Can you take me?"

I want to ask her why she cannot take herself, but then I realise that driving has become too much for her. She is so hesitant and apologetic that I cannot help feeling slightly irritated.

"At the beauty salon?" I ask, distracted by the ringing of my cellphone. My office is calling already.

"Obviously the beauty salon!" she says with aplomb. "What other salon would it be? I'm going in for a checkup tomorrow and I want to look my best."

I am dumbstruck. What need can my mother have for a facial or a manicure at a time like this?

"Sure, Mom," I say. "What time?"

Spinning plates

It saddens me when I realise just how lonely my mother's life is. Where are all her friends? I am amazed at how few lasting connections she has made. For although my mother collects friends and lovers, she seldom keeps them. People arrive in her life and immediately become privy to all aspects of it. Nothing is too intimate. And then, with an equal suddenness, they vanish. It strikes me that my mother is probably too embarrassed to ask her friends for help, although she has been good to them.

I am a good friend too, I guess, thanks to my mother. She raised me to be a nice girl; a good girl. Now I am a woman who never says how she feels. "A lady smiles, no matter what." I want to shout at my mother, Look where being a lady left you! But of course, I say nothing.

Now, as her life nears its end, my mother has no one she feels she can turn to. Is this the natural order of things? Friendships are fleeting, but family lasts forever?

I regret all those years when my life was too busy to call or to visit, although I know I have always been a good daughter to her. I take off work, reschedule my meetings so that I can be there for her. I work late into the night to meet my deadlines. It is no problem; I am used to working late. But first I check that my mother has eaten and taken her medication. It is hard, but I cope.

The routine binds us together. We are closer than we have been in years. We talk, we laugh; we reminisce.

One day, out of the blue, she brings up the topic of my father. If there is one subject that is taboo between us, he is it.

"Your father was young," she says, expressionless. "You must forgive him."

Some people believe that disease is caused by suppressed anger and that just by thinking positive thoughts, you can shrink tumours and reverse illnesses. I am more firmly grounded in reality. I do not entertain such fancies. However, I do know that it would appeal to my mother's sense of melodrama to imagine that somehow, by amassing all her past hurts, she brought this upon herself.

Is her advice a caution not to bring the same upon myself? I cannot really know for sure. This is not a question I can ask. Anyway, my mother likes to throw questions out there and leave me to ponder their importance.

But how can I forgive him? How can we ever change the past? To change the subject, I ask, "What made you marry him?"

"You know that I was pregnant with Lili at the time," she says. "In those days, it was a big thing to have a child if you weren't married. Ma was worried about what people would say, so she insisted that we get married."

"Other people did it," I counter. "Look at Monique and her mother."

"They did not have your grandmother," my mother replies adroitly.

I have heard all this before.

"Did you love him?" I ask.

"Ag, I was young. What did I know about love?"

Summer 1985

The holiday straggles to an end and it is time to go back to school. The baby in her stomach makes my mother so tired that Lili has to walk me to school on our first day back. Then it is assembly and our new teachers are announced. My new teacher is a tall, thin woman with bony fingers and very wrinkled skin. She is called Miss Daniels, even though she is very old. She looks about as old as my ma, I think.

We troop into Miss Daniels's classroom. She surveys us critically as we stand in front of our new desks. Then we have to introduce ourselves to her as she ticks our names off in the register.

During interval, I rush to find Lili. For once she is not rude to me in front of her friends. "Who's your new teacher?" she asks, curious to know. When I tell her, she grimaces and shakes her head wisely.

"Ag shame," she says, "she's a real witch!"

Monique adds, "I think she hates all children."

I'm not sure whether they were trying to scare me, but from now on I think of Miss Daniels as a witch. Especially as she looks like my picture of the witch in *Hansel and Gretel* with her long, pointed fingernails. Why do we need new teachers?

I've been back at school for two weeks when I am called into the principal's office. I am very anxious – being called into the principal's office can mean one thing only: trouble. So I am a bit relieved when I walk into the foyer and see that Lili is already there. Her eyes are wide and strained. Lili approaches the secretary's desk and identifies us.

"Yes," the secretary says, "you must wait for your grandmother. She's coming to fetch you. Get your bags and come back here immediately."

"Excuse me Miss, what is this about?" Lili asks the secretary. "Is it about our mother? Is she alright?"

She doesn't answer. "Just get your bags, girls," she says brusquely. "Your grandmother is on her way."

I nudge Lili as we leave the office. "It must be about the baby, of course. Maybe Mommy had the baby!"

Lili looks at me and smiles. "Yes, of course, that must be why Ma's fetching us."

Ma confirms our suspicions when she comes to fetch us in her large purple Valiant. The baked leatherette seats burn my legs when I plop myself down.

"Your mother has gone into hospital," she tells us. "The baby is coming."

"Who took her to hospital?" Lili demands. "Did an ambulance fetch her?"

"No, of course not," Ma says, turning the car into our road. "She called me. I am her mother, after all!"

Ma has a key to the front door and lets us in. The big hospital bag that was packed weeks ago is no longer at the door. Inside, my mother had put her toiletries and the beautiful black-and-yellow satin nightie and gown set that she bought when she first heard about the baby. We'd watched her as she neatly folded the baby's clothes and placed them in the bag. Babygros and matinée jackets and special blankets called receiving blankets with smiling animals on them and thick bunny blankets in lemon and white. She held each piece to her face and sniffed deeply. I remember this when Ma tells us to pack some clothes because we'll be staying with her while our mother is in hospital. While we are busy, she gets a mop and starts to wipe up something wet and brown on the tiles in the entrance hall. Why hadn't we noticed it when we came in?

♠

When we reach her house, Ma gives me and Lili jobs to do to keep us busy while she makes muffled phone calls in her bedroom with the door closed.

"When are we going to see our mother and the new baby?" Lili demands, but Ma glares at her benignly and tells us that our mother has not had the baby yet. Maybe tomorrow it will have come and then she'll see if we can go. In the meantime, Ma says, we must be good girls and pray for our mother and the baby.

That night, the two of us can barely sleep. We can't wait to see what –

or who – the baby will look like. We are also certain that we won't have to go school during this exciting time.

But of course we do have to go to school. Ma says that she has to go and check up on our mother and that children are not allowed in hospitals. We plead and cajole, but she is firm.

Everyone is curious when I walk into the classroom. For once, Miss Daniels does not scold me for being late. During the break, my friends want to know what happened. They are very disappointed when they hear that the baby hasn't come yet, but they are impressed when I tell them that my mother is in the hospital. Even Miss Daniels wants to know about my mother and the baby.

Ma is quiet when she comes to fetch us from school. Lili and I have so many questions: Is our mother alright? Has the baby come? When can we visit them? She just says, "Quiet, girls, I have to concentrate on my driving. So many questions! Your mother's fine, now be good and let me drive in peace."

Lili and I look at each other and shrug. Ma is like this sometimes and we know better than to argue with her.

After lunch, we are still sitting at the kitchen table when Ma says in her serious voice, "Girls, I have to tell you something."

Concerned, we look at her.

"You know that sometimes things don't work out. Things happen. Sometimes God has other plans . . ."

Lili interrupts before she can finish. "What do you mean, Ma? Is our mother okay?" Lili's voice is slightly hysterical and, taking my cue from her, I start to panic.

"No, your mother's fine," Ma continues. "It's the baby . . ."

"What happened?" Lili presses her. "What's wrong with the baby?"

Ma looks up at us and sighs. "You girls have to be very brave. Your mother lost the baby."

Lost the baby? How do you lose a baby? "Like stolen?" I ask. "Ma, did someone steal the baby?"

Lili answers, "No, like dead. I think the baby is dead. Isn't it, Ma?"

Slowly, Ma nods and holds her arms out to us. Lili shrugs her off and runs outside. I am confused and remain rooted to the spot in the kitchen, idly teasing the worn linoleum with my hard school shoe. Ma gets up slowly and hugs me to her big breasts that smell of baby powder and the lavender soap that she uses. As I sob heartbroken tears, Ma silently weeps. I can tell that she is crying even though she doesn't make a sound because warm tears plop down onto my face. My baby! What will I tell everyone at school tomorrow?

It is the first time anyone I know has died. I was too young when Pa died, although Lili says that she can remember him. Even though I never saw the baby, I knew him. I wanted him.

♠

The next morning, Ma surprises us and says that we don't have to go to school. She will call the principal and explain what has happened. We can stay home and help her.

"We'll go visit your mother later," she says. "Children aren't really allowed into the wards, but I'm sure you can pop in. She wants to see you, but remember, she's still very ill. You have to be big girls, so no crying."

Lili and I nod our heads and agree to everything. We are both desperate to see our mother.

The hospital looks more like a big old house than a hospital. It is in the middle of large grounds, with immaculately trimmed lawns and neat flowerbeds.

"That must be why Mommy chose this hospital," I whisper to Lili. "For the garden." Our mother told us that when she was pregnant with us she'd only look at pretty things, so that Lili and I would be pretty. It was the same with this baby.

Lili does not answer me.

We have to sit in a little room like a lounge while Ma goes in to see our mother. We have picked a bunch of flowers in Ma's garden. Lili and I bicker over who is going to give it to her.

"Ssh," Ma says as she walks away. "Remember that this is a hospital!"

As if in a dream, the two of us flip through the magazines on the little wicker table. Everything is made out of wicker, even the couch and chairs. The room smells of potpourri and hints of furniture polish. There is nothing much in the magazines, mainly pictures and pictures and pictures of happy, healthy babies, which neither of us wants to look at. Lili snorts in disgust and closes the magazines. I mimic her, swinging my legs in anticipation as I wait for Ma to return. There is so much that I want to ask Lili, but she is acting so grown-up that I don't dare. Her eyes are lowered as she stares at her hands, but she has the poise of the ballerina she is.

Eventually, a nurse comes in and says we can go in and see our mother now. We walk down a long corridor to reach her room. Another lady is in the room with her, but she is sleeping, with her back to the wall.

Our mother is propped up in the high bed. She is wearing the beautiful yellow-and-black satin gown that she bought for this occasion. It looks too cheerful for her today. Her face is puffy and her eyes red. What concerns me most are the tubes in her arm and the bag of blood on the metal stand next to the bed. Are they draining her blood? No wonder so many people hate hospitals!

"What is that?" I blurt out, afraid that we'd been tricked and that our mother is more sick than we imagined.

Then something strange happens. Wan smiles crack my mother and Ma's taut veneers. "Oh, this is just a drip," my mother says, and then explains what it is for.

Lili nods wisely, as if she had known what a drip was all along.

"I am so happy to see you girls," our mother says to us. Lili tells her that she's sorry about the baby.

I say, "I'm also sorry about the baby, Mommy, but I'm glad you and Ma are friends again!" Lili gives me a dirty look.

Soon it's time for us to go back to the wicker room so that Ma and my mother can talk in private. As I kiss my mother gingerly on the cheek, she pats my shoulder and whispers, "My baby." I am confused because there is no baby. I am about to ask, but Lili nudges me out of the way and gives my mother a goodbye kiss on her forehead. As we walk out, I remember the most important thing. "When are you coming home, Mommy?"

"Soon," she says.

As we walk back, Lili and I get hopelessly lost. The hospital is much bigger than we imagined. There are too many corridors. Lili leads the way and I follow. There is no one about. Ma said that it was not visiting hours. Eventually we see an old lady ahead. She's standing in front of a glass wall, behind which there are rows and rows of babies in tiny glass cribs.

"That must be the nursery," Lili whispers to me.

Curious, we come to a stop outside the nursery, marvelling at the babies. So this is how they look when they are born, I think to myself. Just like the little pink baby squirrels in my book.

The old lady at the window notices us and smiles. "Which one is your brother or sister, then?"

I start to explain what happened, but Lili interrupts. "We're not sure," she says with a smile. "We don't know yet."

♠

When we get back to her house, we ask Ma for something nice. Doesn't she have chips or chocolates? But Ma does not believe in luxuries. Not even sweets. Not even now. When we ask her for luxuries, she reminds us that she was just a few years older than Lili is now during the war. There were no such things as luxuries then. They were that poor.

"There wasn't enough food to go around," she says with a far-off look on her face. "My mother would send me and my youngest brother, Arthur, to the clinic to get the butter and the cod-liver oil. It was so far to walk, but we couldn't say no. In those days, the government used to sell butter cheap to the poor people and the cod-liver oil had orange stuff floating on top of it, but it kept us healthy."

"Yuck," I exclaim, remembering the time she tried to make me take the cod-liver oil she keeps in the cupboard.

"I thought you didn't like the government, Ma," Lili comments.

"Oh, that was the United Party," my grandmother explains. "It was before this bunch of rubbishes came in."

"Here," she says, offering us sticky blobs of black tamarind. She knows we like the sour taste of this spicy fruit she uses in her curries and we often steal it out of her fridge. As we suck the tamarind, our tongues feeling for the hard seeds, we ask Ma to tell us more about when she was a child, but she looks at us as if she'd just stuck a huge piece of tamarind in her own mouth. "Get your things together – your father's coming to fetch you girls. There's no time for stories."

It is late at night when my father comes. Lili and I are already in our nighties, thinking that he'd forgotten about us. But we didn't dare get into bed in case he came and we were sleeping. This time he doesn't hoot but walks right in. Ma is in the kitchen, making herself a cup of tea before bed.

"I suppose you're happy now?" he spits at her. "Get your things, girls, we're going home," he shouts as he walks out of the house, slamming the front door.

We quickly hug Ma goodbye and Lili says, "Thank you for looking after us, Ma. We love you."

I give her a kiss and then run out. "Daddy, why did you think that Ma would be happy now?" I ask. "Is it because Mommy lost the baby?"

He doesn't answer me.

♠

When we wake up, Ma Matthews is in the kitchen making mielie-meal. This is my absolute worst porridge. Everyone knows that.

"You girls are so spoilt," she says when I tell her that I don't eat mielie-meal. "You'll eat it today, and get done with it or you'll be late for school!"

I look at my father, but he says, "Don't make a fuss, just eat the damned stuff!"

I gulp down the steaming porridge, scorching the roof of my mouth, my only aim to get it down.

"Good girl," Ma Matthews says. "Now get your brush and I'll comb your hair for school."

I was about to correct her and tell her that we don't say "comb" for brushing hair, but something tells me to leave it alone.

She is in her element, attacking the knots in my long hair. "Didn't your other granny comb your hair?" she asks.

I refuse to answer her. Anyway, I liked the ponytails Ma made for me. Even though they are not allowed at school, nobody complained.

After brushing my hair for what seems like an eternity, Ma Matthews grabs a knitting needle and scratches a path down the centre of my head, dividing the hair into two pieces. Then she takes each piece and makes tight plaits that pull on my scalp and make my eyes all squinty. It is painful.

"I look like a Chinese," I exclaim, too scared to say anything else.

It is the wrong thing to say.

"What's wrong with looking Chinese?" she demands. "Don't you know my father, your great-grandfather, was Chinese? You girls know nothing about our side of the family, it seems!"

I am sorry I mentioned it. I am even happy to escape to school and all the questions.

Everyone is awfully nice to me at school, but the strange thing is that no one asks about my mother or the baby.

No one fetches us from school that afternoon. We wait in front, like we usually do when our father is home, but he doesn't come. Eventually Lili grabs my hand and says, "Maybe he's gone to visit Mommy. Maybe he fetched her and brought her home."

We walk home together, a little fast in case she's home.

We can see the car in the driveway when we turn into our road. Having convinced each other that our mother is back home, we run the rest of the way. Panting, we bang on the front door. All is quiet, the only noise a distant song playing in the house. It sounds like the James Taylor record that my mother bought my father for his birthday last year. We carry on knocking, but still no one answers.

Lili says that she'll see if she can climb through a window. She's done this before when our mother lost her keys, but she had been there to boost Lili up until she was perched on the ledge. Now Lili has to launch herself onto the wall that separates our house from the Englishes' and then onto the ledge. It's my job to keep watch for Auntie Ruthie, whom we know will have something to say. We all know how she likes to skinner and since my mother went to hospital, she has been hovering in her front garden, anxious to hear the news. Not that she'd knock on the door and ask! No, all good news must be gathered, like juicy pearls. The harder it is to come by, the more precious it is.

Eventually Lili gets in and opens the door for me. The house is dark and musty because all the windows and curtains are closed. As much as Ma Matthews likes cleaning, the house looks untouched since the morning and now there are plenty more cups and plates joining our breakfast dishes. A burnt pan is still smouldering on the stove.

In the lounge, our father and Ma Matthews are lying snoring on the couch and chair respectively. An empty whisky bottle is standing in a puddle of water on the coffee table in front of them. The one ashtray in the house is choked with cigarette butts. As we survey the scene, Lili and I gasp at the sacrilege: around her legs, Ma Matthews has wrapped one of the baby's bunny blankets, a pale lemon one. If only my mother could see it, she would be so cross!

Lili starts washing up and I dry. We are in no mood for Ma Matthews's nasty comments.

When my father goes to fetch my mother the next day, the bunny blanket is packed away with the rest of the baby clothes. Ma Matthews cleans the house, but not with her normal vigour. As usual, though, she finds ways to snipe at Lili and me; complaining to our father how lazy we are and reminding him of how his sisters have to clean.

"Who does she think cleaned the kitchen yesterday?" Lili asks.

Still, we are in no mood to argue. It doesn't take much to get Ma Matthews going on her litany of how easy we have it. The two of us do our bit, so that if she checks, our mother can see that we've done our jobs. At least when she returns, Ma Matthews will leave.

♠

My mother is sad and stays in her room most of the time. But I think the person who is most upset is my father. He stays in the lounge. Sometimes the TV is off, but most of the time it is on and he stares at it as if transfixed. His eyes do not leave the screen. Even when Lili and I tiptoe softly into the room, he takes no notice, just carries on watching.

The only time he gets up is if he needs to fill his water jug. His bottle of whisky is dangerously low and there are no more bottles in the cupboard. All the Christmas wine is drunk up. I know this because Lili checked and told me so.

Lili makes endless cups of tea for our mother. Sometimes she drinks it. At other times we find the cold, wrinkled tea still in the cup next to her bed.

I struggle to sleep as I try to make sense of all the unhappiness around me. It is the first time I realise that grown-ups can be afraid and that frightens me. I cannot sleep, but I can't climb into the bed with my mother either. I try to count sheep, like my father taught me, but all I see are dead babies – crawling, but still I know that they are dead.

The TV is casting hideous yellow and purple shadows on the wall when I creep out of bed. My father is sitting up with his head in his hands. I sit next to him, hooking his big, hairy arm in my own. Softly I tell him, "Maybe you can teach me to fish, Daddy. I also like to swim and I like soccer. Maybe we can do things."

But my father jerks his arm away. Looking straight ahead he says, "Leave me alone. Go to sleep."

Goodnight girl

I am floored at how quickly my mother's health deteriorates. I visit every day with food, always ready to run small errands and do the things that she is no longer able to do for herself. Things we take for granted, like running to the shops or cutting our own nails. I bring my nail polish and my buffers, shining life into the brittle nails that seem to grow too fast.

"Should I move back in with you, Mom?" I ask.

She thanks me for offering, but says no. She will manage. Although I am reluctant, I realise that I have to give her at least this vestige of independence.

Every night when I leave, I make sure that I have washed the dishes and fed Lady and checked and double-checked the doors and windows. "Have you taken your medicine?" I ask, even if I have seen her do so. It is reflexive.

When I leave, I kiss my mother on her forehead. Sometimes she grips my hand; other times she is sleepy. She still says, "Night, my girl." Just those three words make me feel so safe. They make me feel that I belong somewhere. That this is just temporary. That before long, she will be back to being herself.

Precious moments

I am sleeping when the phone wakes me. My sleep is uneasy and hard won. It takes me forever to fall asleep these days.

"Hello?" I am tentative, expecting the worst.

"Danny . . ." My mother's voice is tremulous, rasping.

"Mom," I say, "what's wrong?"

"Hospital," she breathes. "Need to go . . . hospital."

Naturally, my first reaction is to panic. No matter how much we may imagine that we are prepared and rehearsed, whenever something bad happens, it comes as a shock. Almost a surprise. Whether we had anticipated it or not.

What do I do now? Should I go over? Or would that be wasting time? Should I call an ambulance?

In an instant I am calm. I call the private ambulance service that I checked out before. I have done my homework.

I crook the phone to my ear as I give the dispatcher my mother's address and medical history, hastily flinging on clothes. I am in my car before our conversation ends.

It is that darkest part of the night, just before it starts to get light. The cliché of it being darkest before the dawn pops into my head. I think I now know what it means.

As I drive, the cheesy lines of an old song play over and over in my head – "Is this the beginning? Or is it the end?"

"No, it must be the beginning of the end," I answer myself out loud. The words tumble out unbidden.

The disease is following its predictable course. It is swift. But not too swift.

Autumn 1985

When my father leaves to go back to work, it feels like we can finally expel all the accumulated air from our lungs. We are sad, yet relieved. My father's sadness was oppressive. Infectious. His stay was the longest that I could remember. Longer than Christmas even. Maybe it just seemed so.

♠

"Girls, we need to pull ourselves together," my mother announces to me and Lili as we sit at the lounge table doing our homework.

We look at each other, at a loss. Our mother's animation is unusual. But anything is better than her sadness. She is positive now. Glowing.

"I've decided that I should be a painter," my mother confides, as if bestowing this information on us. "The nuns at school all thought that I had talent. There's a class at the youth centre," she continues conspiratorially. "But it will be our little secret."

"Of course," we agree. We know that our father would not like it.

On the night of her first painting class, my mother dresses like she imagines real painters dress. She wears a new Indian dress shot through with silver and gold thread, with little metal balls that tinkle as she moves. Brightly coloured bangles jangle on her wrists. She will make music wherever she goes.

We are asleep by the time she comes back from the class. But the next morning, she is smiling and making breakfast for us like before.

All in all, she is happier now. At night, we get into her bed and watch TV in her room. We are allowed to bring our Romany Creams and Fanta. Even if we didn't finish our supper. It doesn't matter. Sometimes we fall asleep in her bed and spend the night there.

♠

I am awakened by the loud crash of our lounge window shattering. It is a big window – nearly two metres wide. In my confusion, I am convinced that we are being attacked by burglars. "Lili, Lili," I whisper next to her pillow. "Lili!"

She refuses to wake up. Eventually, I muster up the courage to scurry to the lounge by myself.

My mother is standing motionless in the middle of the room; the brass chandelier above her head casts an eerie shadow over her. I turn on the lights and she is illuminated. My father's golf club suddenly swings in an arc in her hand, then just as suddenly she drops it limply.

"Mommy?"

She looks at me uncomprehendingly.

"Mommy?"

I step closer, mindful of the glass that is everywhere. Shards of glass have fallen on the couch and on the floor. Glass crystals haphazardly cling to my mother's hair. She looks beautiful, like a bride.

Lili joins me in the lounge and we peer into the space where the window used to be. We watch as one by one the neighbourhood lights come on.

Mr English comes over with Auntie Ruthie. What is going on, they want to know. We all do. My mother looks shocked, her eyes far away, as if she's asleep and this is all a bad dream.

Smiling at us vaguely, she mutters, "There was a huge dog . . . I thought it was trying to get into the house."

Lili and I look at each other. Mr English mumbles something under his breath about a man's place being with his family. Auntie Ruthie glares at Mr English. He busies himself by assessing the damage. "Do you know where your father keeps his tape measure?" he asks Lili.

Auntie Ruthie tells me to fetch my mother's gown and steers her towards the kitchen. A cup of sweet tea will be good for her. I shudder as I think about how angry my father will be when he finds out about the window. I hope it will be fixed before he comes home.

My father is in a bad mood when he comes home for the weekend. Not sad, just grumpy. We are learning that it is not always good to have him home. His stays are starting to last longer too, though we do not know why.

The house smells of his socks and we have to be quiet because he's asleep on the couch. My father sleeps a lot when he's home. He hates to be disturbed when he's sleeping. But it is daytime, why should we be quiet? We don't usually make a noise.

Little things are important to my father. Like the amount of television we watch, and the neighbourhood dogs getting into our yard and digging up the lawn. He complains about us leaving our things in the car and if the house looks untidy. Sometimes I watch him running a finger over the windowsills. He says nothing, just sighs and shakes his head.

One Saturday when he is home, my father's friend Uncle Charlie comes to visit. The two of them sit in the lounge drinking their inevitable whisky. My mother is in the kitchen banging pots and furiously executing the meat and vegetables for tonight's supper. I know that she is angry that she had to miss her art class this morning. My father's arrival was unexpected. It seems that she is upset whenever my father comes home these days.

Lili shrugs when I tell her that I'm worried about them. She makes me so cross when she acts like a know-it-all, just because she's older than me. She thinks I know nothing. I'll show her who knows nothing!

I have discovered that if I twirl myself in the heavy curtains in the lounge and stand very still, no one knows that I am there. It's hard for me to stay still for so long, but it's a good hiding place. Not only that, it is a good listening place, and if I look through the small gap between the curtains, I have a good view of the couch.

Uncle Charlie works at the same car plant as my father. His wife, Auntie Karen, and his daughter Janine also live in Cape Town. He and my father travel to work together. This is so my mother can use our car. Since Auntie Karen can't drive, it's Uncle Charlie's car that usually makes the long trip to Port Elizabeth.

"No man, Charlie, I just don't know how long I can go on," my father says, glancing furtively at the door. It is obvious that this is not a conversation for women or children to hear. "Now they've gone and cut our overtime. How are we supposed to support our families?"

Uncle Charlie nods and says, "Right you are, Trevor."

"And the way the darkies are going on in the townships. Those laaities are up to no good, I tell you. Suddenly it's our fault they have no jobs!"

My legs are getting pins and needles. I don't know how much longer I can stand still.

"Ag Trevor, you must see where they are coming from," Uncle Charlie starts. "How they live . . ."

My father looks at him, shocked. "No, Charlie, I didn't figure you for a bloody bleeding heart." My father glares at him, pours two more glasses and plonks one down in front of Uncle Charlie. He downs the other in one swift gulp. The conversation is over for now.

Eventually my father announces that he is going to the toilet. This is my chance! Slowly I edge away from my hiding place, hoping that Uncle Charlie won't see me. I am nearly out of the door when he whispers, "I see you!" Smiling broadly at him, I place my finger on my lips. Uncle Charlie winks at me. It is our little secret.

My father is not one to let things stand. When he comes back from the bathroom, he tries to get Uncle Charlie to see things his way. They are still at it by supper time. As I set the table, I catch snatches of conversation, but it makes no sense to me. My father is so enraged, the conversation continues at the supper table. He shocks us all by telling us (really Uncle Charlie, as we are mere spectators) that he is thinking of quitting his job.

This forces my mother to speak. "You must hang on to your job, Trevor," she tells him. "Look at how many people in the motor industry have lost their jobs already. You are lucky to have a job, the country's in recession and you have a family to consider!"

My father looks at my mother in confusion. She should know better than to speak like this in front of us, in front of Uncle Charlie. After a long silence, he says to her in his most condescending tone, "You don't know what it's like up there, May. The darkies are up to no good in the townships, you must see them go on. It's much worse than over here!"

"I don't like that word," my mother admonishes him quietly. "How must our children grow up – thinking it's okay to use such words?"

My father looks at her, looks at Lili and me; then he carries on. "It's enough our company treats the darkies like they're something special. Ever since that code came in. Why, you should see how many darkies are managers on the assembly line. You'd think we were in America or something! Ask Charlie. And don't talk about the union! I wish I never joined that union – look how they joined forces with the darkies' union. You know, it's a stay-away here, a go-slow there. And who are the ones who lose their jobs? I ask you!" My father slaps his thigh enthusiastically. He is almost animated.

"The country's in recession now, Trevor," my mother tries to explain. "That's why there've been so many lay-offs. That is why you must look after your job. Or must I get a job?"

"May, you know how I feel about my wife working," my father says.

I pay particular attention to my peas.

We make corrections

I have to ask my boss for unpaid leave. Although he is very under-standing at first, his compassion fades when deadlines are pushed back and clients neglected. Soon the message is clear, however subtle: no one is indispensable. Another message I perceive with the hairs on the back of my neck is that people die – everybody does. Deal with it.

How important is it for me to convince women what brand of sani-tary towel to buy or cigarette to smoke at a time like this? They shouldn't smoke anyway! Right now, I cannot worry about market share and consumer-buying behaviour. Demographics come out of my ears. The only statistics I am interested in are survival rates.

Now I go to the hospital every day. Luckily I have some money saved up and can afford to pay my bills and live comfortably. Though I don't know how long this will last.

All my other roles have become insignificant. At other times I may be a lover, a colleague, a friend, but right now I am the daughter of the sick woman. That is all I can concentrate on. And it takes all my efforts to be this. Relationships and work can be resolved later. This is where I am needed.

So smooth

Talking about relationships: the man I have been seeing for the past few months calls me up and asks me to meet him for coffee. I know what this means. We have never met for coffee before. Drinks, certainly, sometimes dinner, but never coffee. He is waiting when I arrive at the coffee shop. Thoughtfully, he has chosen one near to the hospital, but I suppose it is near to his office as well.

"I hate to do this to you," he starts, his eyes focused somewhere between my nose and the wall behind me. "I know that the timing is wrong, but the thing is, I've met someone." Sheepish, contrite.

I look at him in amazement. Did he think I would fall apart at the news? I was under no illusion that he was "the one". I'm not even sure I believe in the concept. Ever since I met him, in a gentler time, I have liked him well enough; but neither of us has tried to convince the other that it was anything more than that.

Poor guy! I look at him with pity. I do not blame him. He seems relieved that I am handling this so well. As if he expected a scene – probably why he arranged this meeting in a busy coffee shop and not in the privacy of my flat, with the possibility of one last time . . . At least he had the decency to tell me himself, instead of fading away.

"Good luck," I tell him and mean it. "I hope you'll be happy."

"You too."

As I leave the coffee shop I allow myself a wry smile. My mother would be happy. Although she had never met him, she always thought that I was selling myself short. I do not have the headspace anyway to entertain the thought of men at the moment. Even if I had the libido.

In the main road, near to Ma's house, there used to be a bridal shop. Lili and I called it the wedding–dress shop. We'd pass it on the way to do Ma's shopping: bread on sale at one shop, cheese a few cents cheaper a kilogram at another. The bridal shop made the long walk to the shops worthwhile. Glamorous. The garish creations with their machine–made lace, sequins and imitation pearls seduced us with their promises of happily ever after.

"That's my one!" Lili would proclaim, asserting ownership of the very dress that I had decided was my favourite.

"No, it's mine," I would squeal in protest.

We could not wait for the new designs to adorn the pouty plastic mannequins with their bouquets of paper flowers in the window so that we could choose our new favourites.

Why should a break–up make me remember this?

How I dearly wish I was not here

I am appalled by the state hospital. What must people think of me, letting my mother stay in a place like this? With nine other women in the ward with her, there is scant privacy. Visitors and patients parade past endlessly. When I happen to make eye contact with these people, I glare at them: my private protest. Some of them smile lukewarm smiles, unsure of how to deal with me; others glare back audaciously. I feel so out of place here, in my expensive clothes and expensive French perfume. I don't care. I have worked hard for what I have.

Everything smells of cheap pine disinfectant, which bears no relation to the real scent of pine at all. The bedding, although clean, has seen better days and is stamped with the initials of the hospital.

"Lili and I can afford to send you to a better hospital," I say loudly, just in case anyone is listening.

"Don't worry about me, this is fine," my mother insists. "This hospital has the best doctors."

There will be no further discussion.

The two of us sit in a loud and uncomfortable silence. I hate this. I need to fill the spaces with words. There has been so much silence between us, for so long. I try again. "Why did he leave his job in the Eastern Cape?" I ask my mother.

"He?" My mother is confused. "Oh, you mean Trevor?" She does not say *your father*. "Let me think." She wrinkles her brow, her eyes squint. "Why don't you let me sit up?" she says, motioning towards the bed for me to crank it up. It is so unyielding that I have to call a nurse for help.

Once she is sitting, she continues: "Where was I?" Memory is becoming increasingly difficult for her now – everything is. But she perseveres. "You must know what it was like in those days," she begins. "In the early eighties, people in the motor industry had good lives. All of them – black and white. Then things started to go wrong again in the country. Remember, there was a drought, recession, sanctions . . ." My mother frowns at the strain of remembering. "Many people lost their jobs. Trevor was one of the lucky ones. But still, he was never satisfied."

"Go on," I urge.

"There had been trouble in the townships for quite a while. If you had seen how the people lived, you would understand why. Some organisation or other called for a stay-away in the area and the unions backed it. I think it was to commemorate what happened in Sharpeville.

"Riots broke out and the police started shooting at the people. I think that something like fourteen people were killed. You must remember! It was in all the papers at the time. There was even a commission of enquiry into what had happened. Lots of things were happening in the Eastern Cape at the time at any rate.

"Trevor told someone that he saw the riots that day. I don't know if it was true. Maybe it was? Anyway, it must have affected him, because soon afterwards, he quit his job. Maybe he wanted to be closer to home."

My mother looks exhausted. She slumps back against the pillows abruptly. I think she is asleep. Then she continues, her eyes still closed.

"I found out years later that the company wanted to put a black man in charge of him. That's probably the real reason why Trevor quit, knowing him – but of course he wouldn't tell me."

Autumn 1985

One day, my father comes home during the week and announces that he has quit his job. It's the Easter school holidays we've all been looking forward to. My mother makes a choking noise: what is he going to do now? My father tells her that his skills are sought after. He is sure he can "walk into another job".

But as the days pass and turn into weeks, it seems that his confidence was misplaced. There are no jobs to be had. Especially in the motor industry. My mother tells him that he should ask for his old job back, but he says that he would rather die than do that. It's funny, money was something that we never heard about before, but now it's all my parents discuss.

My mother says that soon she'll have to get a job, but my father says that no wife of his is going to work. That something will come along soon. My mother snorts and mutters under her breath. Most times my father ignores her, but sometimes he says, "What's that you said?"

"Nothing, dear," she replies.

"I have always supported my family," my father says, "and I'll continue to do so now."

My mother says, so softly that only Lili and I can hear, "You should have thought about that before you quit your job."

To my father, she says, "The country's in a recession, Trevor, there just are no jobs."

This gets my father started on his favourite theme: emigration. "We should leave this country and all its problems, May. Look how well Denver is doing in Australia!"

About a year ago, one of my father's friends emigrated to Australia. My father often phones him there, to my mother's disgust. Overseas phone calls are expensive.

"There are so many jobs there," my father continues. "Denver says I will easily find a good job at his company. And the standard of living!"

"South Africa is my country," is my mother's standard response. "I was born here and my children were born here. There is no way I will leave."

At times our father will try to rope Lili and me into his cause. "Wouldn't you girls like to live in Australia?" he asks. "We'll be so rich, I'll buy us a double-storey."

Lili asks him, "What about Ma? And our friends?"

I say, "What about school?"

Our mother says, "I will not be part of the chicken run and that's final."

Until the next time.

"How come Auntie Astrid left the country?" Lili asks the question that also bothers me. I can't understand how Auntie Astrid could leave her mother and her family behind.

Our mother says, "That was her choice."

My mother doesn't really like Auntie Astrid. I know that. Ma says they haven't spoken in years. When we ask her why, all she does is raise her palms up in the air and says, "I don't know."

Ma tells Lili that it hangs heavy on her heart that her only daughters do not get along. "Sisters should get on," she says.

Weeks pass and still my father does not find a job. He stops shaving and grows stubble to complement his thick moustache – modelled on Magnum PI, whom he likes to think he looks like.

We are not used to our father's man smell. I don't think he bathes every day. He used to be so aware of his looks, but now he wears the same ratty pair of jeans every day – and he smells. I wrinkle my nose at him, but he doesn't seem to notice. Our mother tells me and Lili that he's driving her mad, being in the house all the time. I think I know what she means. It's weird that he is here all the time. The house vibrates with a different frequency now. The air is electrified. I feel like the hairs on my arms and neck are always standing up. My father and my mother don't say much to each other. We live in a house that is silent during the day; the only noise is at night, when the TV casts a flickering and ersatz glow of happy days, American style.

Sometimes he'll go out to drink with his friends, but most times he sits morosely in front of the TV, a glass in his hand and a bottle of whisky next to the chair. Our mother says nothing, yet the bitterness and resentment glow in her eyes. She is like a caged animal with our father around. A wild, caged animal. She is forever pacing the passages of our house. Stalking, trying in little ways to reclaim her space. Never succeeding.

With our father here, she seldom leaves the house. The art classes are a thing of the past. Lili and I look on, bewildered. We don't know what to do.

At night we hear loud hisses from the bedroom; sometimes our father flings the heavy door open and stomps out of the room, down the passage to the lounge, where he turns on the TV. Loud. Even though we are already in bed and it's school tomorrow. Yet he is the one who insists that we are in bed by eight o' clock!

Suddenly, in the middle of all this, there is some good news – or at least, Lili and I think so. Our mother tells us that tomorrow we don't have to go to school.

"Is it a holiday?" Lili wonders.

"Something like that," my mother replies.

"What's this now?" my father wants to know as he catches the tail end of the conversation.

"It's nothing, Trevor, just another stay-away."

"For what?" he demands, as if my mother is the one who called the stay-away.

"May Day, Trevor. They asked the students to stay away."

"What?" my father bellows, his face rapidly turning pink and then red. "What do you mean, the girls must stay away from school just because some idiot says so?"

"Everyone's doing it, Trevor. Do you want the girls to be the only ones at school?"

My father walks away, at a loss. "I'm warning you, May," is all he says.

The next day we do not go to school.

I will be your friend

I am a private person. I have never felt comfortable unburdening myself – to friends or strangers. When things become difficult I cope. I hate asking for help. Now, I have to let go of all of this.

As children, we learnt to keep to ourselves. Our house was big and where we lived, big meant beautiful. Our friends would talk wistfully about our "beautiful" house, but Lili and I stopped inviting them over. Only Monique persevered. Tracey and I stopped being friends at some point. There was no rule forbidding having friends over, but still, the reluctance was there. I could not risk them coming. We never knew what to expect when we came home. On most days, we would come in and our father would be lying on the couch. Depending on his mood, he might open his eyes and greet us. But most days he pretended to be asleep. I never knew anyone to sleep as much as he did.

Now, I am humbled and not a little amazed by the outpouring of support that comes from all directions. My friends take turns to see that I am fed, and that the mundane things that need to be done are done. The things that I do not have the time or the inclination to do.

One of my colleagues who lives near my mother's house regularly waters the garden and collects the mail for me. I don't know what to do with the unopened mail, so it accumulates in my cubbyhole until one day it spills out of there too. I do not want to invade my mother's privacy, but I open the envelopes with windows – bills, which I settle myself. Not that there is much to pay. Very little water and electricity gets used, since my mother is elsewhere.

I agonise over the question of Lady, my mother's ageing dog. My building does not allow pets and I'm not that fond of her anyway. She is old, I rationalise, people put their pets down every day; but I cannot do that. Certainly, it would upset my mother. I definitely cannot do that to my mother. She asks about that damned dog every day. Luckily, Charlene, who waters the plants and collects the mail, offers to take Lady in. I am so relieved that I agree immediately. It takes much courage for me to relay the news to my mother. How she loves that miserable scrap! It has always been her nature to collect strays that nobody else wants.

"Does this Charlene have children?" my mother asks. When I acknowledge that she does, my mother says, "Lady will like that."

The concern of my friends, and also of people I regard myself as merely acquainted with, overwhelms me. Some of them phone just to find out if I am coping.

Am I that giving? I must honestly concede that I am not. I feel ashamed of how self-absorbed I've been. The things I overlooked, the people I refused to see. I am the kind of person who avoids my friends if I think they need me. I am scared of saying the wrong thing. Scared of their expectations. I make deals with myself: If I get through all of this, I will change. I will be a better person.

So far away

Lili phones me every night for an update. Sometimes she leaves a message on my cellphone, which is almost permanently switched off during the day now. The cheerful clanging ringtones are out of place in the hospital, where I spend most of my time. I go to sleep with it on though, just in case.

I can hear the phone ringing as I open the door of my flat, but I won't make it in time. Instead, I pour myself a drink and wipe out an ashtray; wait for the phone. As soon as I sit down, having just lit a cigarette, it goes again. I let it ring a bit longer as I compose myself, take a deep breath and prepare for my sister's voice on the other side of the world.

"Hi?" Lili says, annoyingly quizzical and bright. "How is she?"

I do not know how many times our conversations have started this way. It's never, "How are you?" It is always our mother's welfare that we are concerned about.

"The same," I reply, "no worse."

"Hell, I wish I could be there . . . you know that, don't you, Danny?"

I make murmuring noises and tell her what she wants to hear. I reassure and understand. Work's tough and so on. That I know she cares.

I draw deeply on my neglected cigarette, burning away in the ashtray on my lap. Lili hears it immediately. "I can't believe you're smoking!"

It is more than a month that I have been smoking again. The Camel Lights are an easy habit to cling to in times like these. I will stop when it's over, I convince myself. I've stopped before.

I don't even try to explain, and the distance between us stretches even further.

"Should I come home?"

Instead of answering her, I tell her that our mother is stable, and that she needs to be strong right now. I tell her that I know she would be here if she could. But saying the words does not diminish my resentment. I am trying to muster all my exhausted resources while my indispensable sister has bigger things to worry about: the global economy, unemployment. Other people and their problems.

We chat desultorily; we are so good at this polite talk. I hear about her new car and we ponder whether it was the right choice. She's not sure about the colour. I wonder who needs a car in London. Did I see her on the news? Someone told her that she'd made the South African news for some important deal she had been part of. Then she tells me about the deal and also what she wore to the press conference. I tell her that I missed it, but that I'm sure she looked good. I end the conversation by telling her that I'll call if anything changes. That she should try to get some sleep.

Like normal

Lana, one of my oldest friends, has been around to my place and left notes and messages. She has avoided the hospital, however, as have most of my friends. I understand this and prefer it. I know why people stay away. Hell, it is what I would do.

It is so easy to overlook people who are ill. First we convince ourselves that it is not serious, that they will soon get better, come home from hospital. We'll visit them then, when our lives are not as hectic, when we really have the time. Meanwhile, there are work pressures, deadlines, husbands, children, other commitments. It is easy to put things off.

Lana turns up at my flat one Saturday morning.

"Come, we're going shopping," she announces. "Get dressed," she instructs me, taking in my skanky tracksuit pants and shapeless, colourless T-shirt. "YDE's having a sale, didn't you get the SMS? And Richard's going to look after the kids."

In another world, things like this would have mattered to me. Clothing sales, trying on make-up and browsing for books. (A good place to meet men, since at least you know that they read.) Later, we'd go for lunch and get tipsy on wine – or if we're feeling really decadent, cocktails.

My look says it all. I don't need to say anything.

"Forget about the sale," Lana soothes. "Why don't you have a shower while I make us some breakfast?"

Refreshed by the final blast of cold water in the shower, I sit at my kitchen counter while Lana lays out the bacon and scrambled eggs. There are tomatoes, fried the way I like them. She must have gone down to the shops while I was in the shower. I haven't bought fresh vegetables in weeks.

"I know, I'll go with you to visit your mom!" Lana suggests bravely.

I look at her with such gratitude that my, "It's not necessary, you really don't have to . . ." is met with a firm rebuttal.

"Of course I do, I love her too, you know."

All my friends loved my mother when we were growing up. She was so beautiful, and much younger than all the other mothers. The girls would confide in her, as she offered the best advice regarding boyfriends and other issues that are important to teenage girls. But I could never confide in her. Neither could Lili, I think. Around her, we'd be stars – capable, sensible, intelligent. Beyond all those things like falling in love or having your heart broken. Sometimes, she'd tease me, trying to get me involved in the conversation, to get my friends to reveal my secrets. But what seemed so easy to them was unnatural to me.

"I'm not interested in boys," I'd proclaim, as if such things were beneath me.

Later, when the girls left, my mother would grimace at the foolishness of my friends. Make gentle fun of them and their problems. But they never knew.

The stranger in the bed

I find myself at the sale, but I don't buy anything. For once, clothes in the size I normally wear fit loosely on me, but I am uninspired. We stop at the expensive flower shop in the mall so that Lana can buy my mother a large bunch of flowers. I am grateful that she remembers that tulips are her favourite flowers – or maybe it is just a coincidence.

As she drives, I try to prepare her.

"She's not the same," I volunteer. "Don't be surprised."

Lana looks at me out of the corner of her eye. She is a cautious driver. Her eyes do not leave the road. "Of course – I know she's very ill."

Still, I don't think that she's prepared for the sight of my mother lying there. As we walk through the depths of the state hospital, looking very out of place, I can see that Lana is girding herself for the experience. Although it takes us about ten minutes to get to the ward – the lifts are erratic and insufficient – I can't help but think that it's not enough time for Lana to prepare herself.

The hospital is busy – we have come during visiting hours. People jostle us in the lift. Don't breathe on me, I think to myself, shocked by the poverty and desperation of many of the patients and visitors. Lana's nose crinkles up at the hospital smell, but I find that I am used to it.

My mother is sleeping when we get there. I think if I had not walked to the bed, Lana would not have picked her out in the general ward.

She opens her eyes as we approach the bed, smiles feebly at Lana in misty recognition. I can see Lana's shock as she takes it all in, hear her swallow hard next to me. The woman in the bed bears no resemblance to the woman she knew and expected.

Looking at my mother through her eyes, I take in the shrunken body. It is as if she has been compacted. Her skin is ashen. Her eyes and nose appear larger in the fleshless face.

I inwardly wince at the condition of her mouth. It is covered in sores, and I automatically search my bag for some lip gloss. Only once I find the nearly full tub of strawberry-flavoured lip gloss do I worry about germs. My germs. But I apply it anyway; the cracked lips must be painful. I leave the tub next to her bed.

Lana is visibly shaken. Trying hard to be brave for my and my mother's sake. While I am busy attending to my mother's meagre toilette, Lana walks to the window and gazes out into the far distance, still clutching the tulips. Please don't let her cry, I intone over and over in my head as I cleanse my mother's face and apply moisturiser.

I call a nurse over to help me crank up the bed. Once my mother is upright, I spray some of her favourite perfume on her wrists and neck. It is an old trick of mine: wearing perfume to feel better.

"All ready," I say brightly, "Lana, my mom's ready for you now!"

Lana takes her cue from me and also busies herself. She arranges the flowers in an empty vase that the nurses have brought over unnoticed.

I catch her surreptitiously sniffing the tulips – searching for a fragrance to block out the hospital smell, I think.

I dutifully bring flowers once a week, yet a part of me thinks that there is something incongruous about flowers in this ward. The yellow tulips, especially, look out of place. They are happy flowers. Flowers for celebrations. Not this. It takes a long time before Lana is happy with the way the flowers are arranged. Only then does she turn her attention to my mother.

"I'm sorry I never came sooner . . . Richard, the kids . . ." she explains. I feel that it is to me that she is trying to explain. To apologise for having a life removed from this. For having no real need to be here.

I wonder if she is going to tell my mother that she's looking better and will surely be going home soon, as do most of my mother's visitors. Reassuring themselves more than her, I think, with the lie. It is the done thing to say; to give the patient hope.

Unexpectedly, Lana says, "I'm so sorry to see you like this. It breaks my heart."

As her voice cracks, again I silently beseech her not to cry. I don't think I can handle it. We have to be brave at times like these.

My mother struggles to speak. Finally, once I've coaxed a few droplets of water down her throat, her voice that is not her voice croaks, "Good girls . . ."

Uttering just these two words requires all her effort. She collapses against the pillow, exhausted. She is so easily tired, lapsing in and out of wakefulness as we hover around the bed. The visitors at the other beds in the ward look at us sympathetically. My mother is the most ill patient in the ward and, out of respect, everyone talks softly and looks away from her inert form.

Visiting hours are over and we have to leave; Lana has been away from her family for most of the day. I kiss my mother goodbye on her forehead and so does Lana. It is only in the car that Lana allows the tears to gush out.

"I'm glad I came, but facing her was one of the hardest things I've had to do," she confesses. "How do you manage?"

I shrug wordlessly. I am her daughter. I have no option.

Autumn 1985

As autumn fades, the heat is stifling. Winter is a long way off. For someone who has left Port Elizabeth, my father is awfully interested in what
happens there. He scours the papers to learn what is going on in the
place that he called home for as long as I can remember. He doesn't
have to look hard. It's on the front page of all the newspapers. As my
father says, "There's always something happening in the Eastern Cape.
And all of it bad." But he doesn't explain what he means.

Every day at school, after we say Our Father, it's news time. Most
children talk about birthdays, a new bike, a puppy. When my mother
told me about the baby, it was big news. The kind that everyone wants
to tell and everyone wants to hear about. I never told anyone about her
losing the baby. Everyone knew, but no one talked about it. Once,
Linda in my class told me that her mother also lost a baby, but that
was the only time that anyone spoke about it to me. I don't remember
what I said.

Whenever the teacher asks who has news, I put my hand up. I always
have news, because I read the newspapers every day and watch the TV
news. But Miss Daniels asks the other children for their news. Even
those who don't put up their hands.

One day, Miss Daniels tells the class that she doesn't want to hear news news. The papers are full of bad news, she explains, and children shouldn't read them. She says that we should talk about what happens to us or our families. I don't understand this, because last year, Miss Cupido, my Sub A teacher, was always interested in what I had to say. It was because of her that I started reading the newspapers. Maybe Miss Daniels just doesn't like me.

We do not have a dog, though my mother says that all children should grow up with a dog. My father doesn't want a dog. He says it will mess up the garden, and who'll be the one to clean up after it? Him, that's who.

I pray and pray that God will send me a dog for my birthday. Miss Daniels says that if we pray out loud, God will hear our prayers and answer them. If we are good, that is. This is because God watches over us every day. For weeks and weeks I pray for a dog and am very careful to be good. It's just like before Christmas.

On the morning of my birthday, I wake up all wound up, certain that God has heard my prayers. Before anyone can wish me, I run outside to check whether God has sent me a dog down from Heaven. But there's nothing there. I am so disappointed.

"Here boy, here girl . . ." I whistle, but there is no welcoming bark, no wagging tail.

My mother comes outside when she hears me call. "Come here, my girl," she says. "Happy birthday. Now get done for school. I'm sure that your present will be here when you get back."

At school, everyone looks at me expectantly when it's time for news. My birthday is proudly displayed on the birthday chart for all to see.

"Don't you have any news, Danika?" Miss Daniels asks after the class has sung "Happy Birthday" to me.

"No, Miss Daniels," I say softly. Everyone knows that I want a dog.

I walk home in misery, but when I get there, my mother is waiting at the gate with the cutest, licketiest yellow puppy in her arms.

"Look what came while you were gone," my mother says. "It's a boy!"

"God really did answer my prayers!" I squeal in delight and vindication.

Lili gives me a queer look, but says nothing.

"What are you going to call it?" my mother asks.

"What about Boomer?" I say. "I always liked that name."

My mother makes me a chocolate cake with pink icing. We each have a piece after supper. Tomorrow I will take Ma a slice when I go fetch my present. My father doesn't complain about the puppy at all.

It is a very happy birthday.

Better days

My mother can no longer eat. She is being fed intravenously. I am nau-
seated by watching the nurse insert the thick mixture into the tube.
This is the only nourishment my mother is getting. She has always
enjoyed her food. Now food is pared down to its basic function: to keep
her alive. There is no joy in eating here, for her or for me.

I rack my brain trying to think what I can make for her. Something
sapid and easily digestible. I contemplate stewing food and puréeing it,
but that reminds me too much of baby food. I cannot do that to my
mother. I would make her a vegetable soup, like butternut or even
beetroot, though I know that she does not like such things. So I make
her sweet watermelon sorbet. I am absorbed in the chopping of the
watermelon into cubes. Concentrate on mixing and blending. I am so
hopeful – my mother has always liked watermelon. If I can take her
this smell and taste of summer, perhaps it will make her feel, just for
the moment the watermelon touches her lips, that she is living and not
merely existing.

Perhaps it will remind her of the days when we would buy a big
watermelon and take it to the beach, icy cold from being kept in the
fridge overnight. When we'd leave early in the morning and come home

late at night, so tired that we'd fall asleep in our bathers. Perhaps she will remember how she taught us to swim in the Camps Bay tidal pool, even though she could not swim herself.

The nurse suggests that I ask the doctor whether my mother can eat the sorbet, in case it does not agree with her. As I tell the doctor the ingredients, I register his patient bemusement. From his expression, I can tell that it doesn't matter to him what I give her or what it contains, as long as it does not make her worse. The slight nourishment of the sorbet will not reverse her condition. Dehydration and lack of food are the least of her problems, his look says.

I get a bowl and a spoon from the kitchen and take it over to my mother. Her eyes flutter in recognition when she sees me. Her face tries to form a smile. I can see that it is a good day. She motions that she wants to sit up. I call a nurse over to help. Once she is sitting, I tell her about the sorbet that I have made. Remind her how much she loved watermelon. I spoon a bit into her mouth. Amazingly, it goes down. My mother's face is rapturous. I spoon a little more, but she is not able to eat much. The watermelon melts on her lips and dribbles. The frustration shows on her face. Once more, her body is letting her down. "Watermelon," she whispers before she falls asleep.

I sit watching my mother sleep. Just sit there. When she wakes, she looks around, confused. I am here, I say. I tell her the fairy tale of how she is going to get better and what we will do when she leaves this place. She nods weakly. Her mouth manages to form a smile, but her eyes do not meet mine.

Just to hear you breathing

My mother's soft breathing lulls me to sleep. I am amazed that I am able to sleep through all the activity of the hospital. The noise of the other women in the ward. A while back, I figured that this was the reason for keeping all the patients drugged up. So they could get some sleep. How I long for just one night of undisturbed sleep!

When I wake, my first instinct is to check on my mother. I stand over her inert form. She is still breathing. As I stand there and watch her sleep, her breathing is almost indiscernible. Gentle, even reassuring. The memory comes to me of how, as a child, I would always check to see if my mother was alive when I found her sleeping. Before I learnt not to do so, I would flap open her eyelids to see if she was still there. I don't know what I expected – a chasm, a void in the sockets where the eyes should be? Children can be so macabre.

Later, I learnt to check her breathing: the rise and fall of her chest, the characteristic twitch of her nose. I would hover over her to make sure, until she woke up. Most times, she would be furious at my intrusion. I certainly would be.

A nurse comes over hesitantly – they must have seen that I had been sleeping. It is time for another feed; time for her medication. The nurse touches my mother lightly on the cheek. She does not stir. Still, I know that she is alive. I checked her breathing. The nurse looks at me swiftly, trying to hide her alarm.

"I'm going to call Doctor," she informs me in that slightly obsequious way unique to medical staff when they refer to doctors. "Doctor will know what to do."

I am still not concerned. My mother is fine. Her breath is even and not laboured. Most of all, it is there. I stand over her, watching and waiting. Willing her to wake.

After a short while, the young doctor comes in, not quite breathless, not quite rushed. Business as usual.

"Stand back, please," he says, staccato. I watch attentively as he does a few tests, trying to get a response from my mother. Her knee jerks reflexively, but she does not wake. His back is towards me and for the merest second he stands that way, not doing anything, just standing. Then he turns around.

"I'm sorry to tell you this, but it seems that your mother has lapsed into a coma."

His voice is bland. It contains no inflections. This must be his practised bad-news voice.

I gasp. This is all happening too soon. I look at him, searching for the answers to questions I do not know how to articulate.

"This happens often with this disease," he says more gently – a bit more human. He places his arm awkwardly around my shoulder, offering me some meagre comfort. I am grateful for this little bit of kindness as I sink down into the chair. A few minutes ago, I had been checking my mother's breathing . . .

Now that I think about it, I don't believe I ever grew out of checking to see that my mother still breathed. If she slept for too long, Lili and I would both tiptoe into her bedroom. No matter how quiet we were, she would always wake up.

Why doesn't it work now?

A waking dream

Someone decides that it is best if my mother is moved to one of the private rooms opposite the ward. On the other side of the nurse's station.

Best for whom? I want to scream, but remain silent. I am learning the rules of the hospital.

The room is just big enough for the bed. There are two reasonable armchairs on either side. A window looks out onto the adjacent buildings. The best thing about the room is the clean hand-basin and the dispenser of liquid disinfecting soap attached to the wall. I have been washing my hands in the bathroom attached to the general ward. A necessary evil.

Once my mother is settled in, I lower myself onto one of the leatherette armchairs. Somehow I get through the day. Then, mercifully, it is time to go home. To eat, listen to my messages, take my mind off things. Sleep.

Easier said than done.

I try to forget about today, but I cannot. I know that it is some kind of watershed, but it is better if I treat it like any other day in the course of my mother's illness. I long for the oblivion of sleep. Perhaps a glass of wine will help. But of course I don't stop there. I drink the one remaining bottle of wine in my flat until there are only dregs left. At least I didn't finish it, I console myself. Yet I know that if there were another bottle, I could drink it.

Still, I lie awake. The alcohol does not help me sleep. I will phone Lili tomorrow. Right now I need my sleep.

I am running. The crowd surges and scatters. All running. Hundreds of us running. A confusion of running. The air is filled with the bitter stench of smoke and sweat. Clouds of dust engulf us. I struggle to see. I push forward. Afrikaans voices boom and blast: "Daar's hulle!" I need to get away. My legs buckle. I steady myself. The blood is pounding in all my veins. I gasp for air, choking.

The noise is the worst. People are wailing in their terror and disbelief. We are surrounded. The momentum pushes us forward. Past the men with dogs and guns. Past the huge trucks that are blocking the road. The feared sjamboks rain down, flailing desperately to make contact with skin. Survival instinct replaces the spirit of solidarity: we jostle and trample one another to get away.

I wake up drenched in sweat, my breath struggling in gasps. I switch on the light and check my watch. Five past four. I could have guessed – it is the time I wake up every morning now. Outside, the world is dark; people asleep. I know that I will not sleep, but I will not get up either. To get up would be to admit defeat. Instead, I switch pillows, taking the cool, unused pillow from the other side of my bed. I pull the blankets around tighter, then kick a leg out. I try counting – not sheep, just counting. My mind races and blocks out the counting. Sleep, come.

All we have left unsaid

Why didn't you tell us more? Why did you try to protect us? We knew, but we didn't know. I hate that this hackneyed excuse is mine too. I guessed. And so I feared. Better to put a name to it. I was intelligent. I would have understood. Instead, the unknown grew into bigger and bigger fears. Our only source of information: listening in on adult conversations or watching the TV news. Sometimes we would find the newspapers that you hid away. But these weren't reliable sources, were they? Not at the time.

I have so many questions, and now I fear it is too late.

Winter 1985

As autumn limps to a close, my mother speaks about an Indian summer. Then the floods come. It rains without stop for many days. My mother says that we are lucky to have a roof over our heads, as many homes have been washed away in the townships. The TV news shows the flooding. Streets look like rivers; people wade across, trying to rescue their belongings. A man and a boy, pants rolled up above their knees, paddle a makeshift boat in a water-swollen street. I am too clever to say what I really think. That it looks like fun.

After the floods, the snow comes. When we are on the bridge coming from Ma's house, we can see the white layer on the top peaks of the Hottentots Holland range. Dazzling white, it reminds me of the Swiss Alps where Heidi lives with her grandfather. Our mother tells us that there's snow on Table Mountain this year, so we really freeze. It is so cold that our mother makes Lili and me push our beds together for more warmth. I find this thrilling, even a bit dangerous. I sleep with my socks on. My mother says that if your feet are warm, you will be warm, no matter what. Lili scoffs at my thick, warm socks when I come to bed. "Don't touch me with that," she warns. "Keep to your side!"

As soon as there is a nip in the air, my father makes his huge pots of soup in the black cast-iron potjie. The boiling soup fills the air with its smell of burn. If the smell of the soup simmering on the stove is bad, the taste is worse. We struggle to get it down. All the vegetables in the house go into it, as well as soup bones and dog-food bones. A layer of scum coats the pot, which is a nightmare to clean. The soup is thick and floury. Our mother says it's because my father doesn't cook the split peas properly, but she eats it anyway. We all do, smacking our lips and making noises of enjoyment.

The fire is another winter ritual. As soon as the air turns cold, before night falls, our father makes a fire in the Jetmaster that he installed. You can tell he did it himself, because the area around the fireplace is still unfinished and the flue doesn't work properly. So the smoke settles in our hair, our clothes and the furniture until we feel we can't breathe. The heat is sultry and oppressive. I long to fling open the doors and windows to let the fresh air in, no matter how cold it is.

Every winter, our mother buys us new winter clothes: spencers, pyjamas, slippers, a new winter gown if we've outgrown last year's and a new school tracksuit. This year, we will have to make do with all our things from last year, as there is no money. When we complain, our mother says, "Remember there are people worse off than you." We don't believe her and tell her so. She reminds us of the people left homeless by the flood – but they are just people on the TV screen.

To prove her theory, she takes me and Lili to the outskirts of the townships so that we can see how other people live. We are shocked that people can live packed so closely together and not in real houses, just collections of wood and tin. There are rows and rows of toilets. They look as if they've been planted in the field by some crazy farmer. But mainly I notice the mud. And the dirt. And the straggly goats that wander in the road among the children, who play the same kind of games I play with my friends at home. Except, of course, we play with dogs instead of goats.

"Slow down, Mommy!" Lili warns as a stray dog darts in front of us.

"Yes, why don't you stop the car?" I suggest, wistfully looking at the games.

"We can't stop here," our mother tells us. "It's not safe."

"Why not?" I ask, watching the children play.

"People are unhappy," our mother explains. "And unhappiness can lead to strange things."

Quietly, Lili says, "I can't blame them if they are unhappy."

That night I pray extra hard for the people living there. Maybe we are a bit lucky after all.

It gets dark very early now. If the curtains are closed, you don't realise just how dark it is outside. We have to scramble outside to bring in the washing when the first drops of rain start to fall like fat pebbles. There are no stars: heavy rain clouds obscure the sky. The world seems smaller, denser, more menacing. I feel like Chicken-licken.

One day, Uncle Charlie and a few of my father's other old friends come to visit, bringing their expensive whisky with them. The kind that my father used to buy before. My father shouts at my mother to make them some food. Bravely and stupidly, my mother goes into the lounge and says that there is no food in the house.

"Then get some," my father says in his cold, mean voice.

"You know there's no money, Trevor," my mother says. In front of everyone.

My father's eyes narrow dangerously and his nostrils flare as he stares at my mother, his face red.

"But you men enjoy your expensive whisky," my mother says brightly to the company, then walks out.

I stay outside the door, curious to see what will happen now. Uncle Charlie gets up and says, "Trevor, I think we should go. It's obvious May's not happy."

"Stay," my father insists. "This is my house."

"Some other time, hey?" Uncle Charlie says, motioning for the others to go.

"Why don't you come with us to my place, hey, Trevor?" one suggests.

"Sure, sure," my father says, trying to regain his composure.

Uncle Charlie leaves the room and finds my mother sitting at the kitchen table. "Here," he says to her softly, handing her a fifty-rand note. "Take it for the children. I'm sorry that it's not much, but it's all I have on me."

My mother takes it and stuffs it into the pocket of her jeans.

Uncle Charlie looks around when he sees me at the door. He and my mother look at each other guiltily. They are lucky that I am not my father. I am relieved too, but also a bit nervous.

♠

Our father is livid when he gets back home: defiant, looking for a fight. He enters the house like a tempest; Lili and I run out of our room when we hear the front door slam. We are prepared for this. Since he left, we have been anticipating his return.

He smells cloudy like cigarette smoke and his breath is thick and sour from the whisky. Lili and I follow behind him cautiously as he stalks around, looking for our mother. He takes no notice of us.

She is sitting up in bed, trying to read, when he finds her. Our mother appears to shrink against the headboard as he strides towards her. This is a side of him that we have never seen before, nor imagined. He pushes her up against the headboard, his fist shoved drunkenly under her chin.

"Woman," he slurs, "don't you *ever* embarrass me in front of my friends again!"

Lili and I stand ashen-faced in the passage. I am so scared to see my father act like this. Lili takes a few tremulous steps into the room, but I remain where I am.

Giving her a final poke in the chest, he picks up the car keys he dropped as he came into the room. Without saying a word, he storms past us and out of the house, the tyres screeching as he pulls away.

I hope that the neighbours haven't heard. What must they think?

Happy birthday to you

Today is my mother's birthday. In honour of the occasion, I decide to bake her a cake. When my mother was unhappy, she would devour loaves and loaves of white bread, thickly smeared with butter and peanut butter. For me, it is cake. Preferably one I have baked myself.

It is so reassuring, the creation of a cake. You measure out the ingredients, then cream, whisk and fold to meld them together into something delicious. As I beat the batter, I regret all the times I deprived my mother of the pleasure she used to derive from my baking. "No one makes better cake than you," she'd say. But then she was diagnosed with diabetes and, as with a naughty child, I'd refuse her a slice. "You must watch your sugar," I'd admonish. "Do you want to die?"

Now if only I could give her a slice of this beautiful cake! It is chocolate, her favourite. I beat together cream and cooled melted chocolate to make a ganache topping. The inside is pure chocolate buttercream, and I pipe rosettes of this on top as well. I crumble up a bar of Flake and sprinkle it over the surface. Jaunty, bright red maraschino cherries complete the look. My mother would love this cake!

I consider taking it to the hospital. Perhaps if she saw this beautiful cake she would realise that it was her birthday. "Happy birthday, Mom, look what I made you!" I'd say. "Make a wish!" Then I'd ask the nurses for some forks and we'd eat our cake like we used to, speculating about what the year ahead had in store. Perhaps if she saw all the love I'd put into the cake, she would wake up for me. Like magic.

Looking at my work of art, I am half convinced I should take it with me. But I imagine the pitying looks of the nurses and stop myself. Instead, I cut myself a large slice and say, "Here's to you, Mom!"

Before I know it, I have eaten almost half of the cake. Many happy returns.

Bulletproof

Though I eat, occasionally gorge myself, I – who have always been on a diet – no longer have to watch my weight. The few unwanted kilos I fretted about in the past drop off me effortlessly. Not that this brings me much joy. I marvel at the person I once was: concerned with my appearance and desperate to follow the latest trend. Perhaps my job did that to me, but I know that it is more than this.

How can I now worry about extraneous things, like whether laser therapy or electrolysis is better for hair removal? How can I agonise about whether a high- or low-protein diet is better suited to my particular body make-up?

Once upon a time, I was smug that there were no dread diseases in my family, that my relatives all died of old age – as if this were evidence of my good genes and indestructibility. It allowed me to smoke for many years, assured that I was not predisposed to cancers. Eat whatever I wanted. The only constant eating pattern in my life, for as long as I can remember, has been yo-yo dieting.

Now I have to reassess my life, my beliefs. Along with the diabetes, I have to concern myself with the possibility that I am at high risk for this disease. It is so obscure that doctors are not even sure if it's genetic. I have to take vitamin pills and try to exercise. I have to try to eat five servings of fruit and vegetables a day. I am no longer bullet-proof.

Blood is thicker than water

Auntie Astrid turns up at the hospital unexpectedly. I wasn't even aware that she knew my mother was sick. I wonder who let her know.

"You naughty girl," Astrid trills, a touch too brightly for our surroundings, "why didn't you call me?"

I look at her in astonishment. It had honestly not occurred to me.

Seeing the puzzlement on my face, Astrid grips my hand in that earnest North American way of hers. "It's okay, honey," she says in her shrill not-quite-Canadian-not-quite-South African voice. "I'm here now, okay?"

I don't know whether she and my mother have been on speaking terms recently. But then I realise that either way, Astrid would do the

right thing. Like my mother, she believes that appearances are everything.

I remember the first time Astrid came back for a visit. In the honey-
moon days of the new South Africa. "I wouldn't set a foot back here
until the country was free, dahling!" she proclaimed to me in her stri-
dent tones.

I thought of asking her whether she was politically active, but knew
the answer. We were all on our best behaviour. My mother was contrite. Although, when they thought no one was looking, the two of them
sat at opposite ends of Ma's kitchen table, glaring at each other. When
anyone glanced over at them, their faces would become smooth and
unreadable. Blank of any emotion. It was hilarious, these two older
women acting like petulant teenagers. It was strange to see my mother
as a sister.

My grandmother was very excited to have her daughter back, even
if Auntie Astrid insisted on staying in a guesthouse and not her childhood home. She should have saved her money: she spent most of her
time there anyway, revisiting her old haunts, seeing whether she could
still inflame the passions of the boys of her youth. They called to invite
her out – I would find her giggling on the phone. I doubt whether any
of their wives came along.

She reminded me of my mother then, all flirty and girly around men,
although she did take more care of her appearance. One morning she

asked me to accompany her to the hairdresser down the road, as she wanted her hair blown out.

"It's important that we take care of ourselves," she advised me. "You must always look your best when you go out – you never know who you'll meet."

I felt that she was constantly appraising me, but with the insouciance of youth, I was unaffected. And it didn't bother me too much that she constantly compared "Cannadaa" to South Africa – always favourably. Everything was bigger and brighter and more advanced in her adopted country. She was particularly vocal about the number of television channels available, and could not believe that we could be happy with the few we had.

Of course, my mother found a lot to sneer about, telling no one in particular, "Well, we may not have fifty TV stations, but at least we have things like sunshine here. We're real people – we haven't forgotten who we are!"

But I was fond of Astrid, in my own way. She told ribald stories of when she and my mother were younger, and I was glad to hear about a woman I had never known existed. I thought it a great pity that they were no longer close. Especially as Astrid ("Please! *Auntie* makes me sound ancient!") said that they'd been very close when they were younger. Although my mother was being stonily polite for Ma's sake, that's all she was. There was no warmth in her relationship with her sister; the distance between them seemed impossible to bridge. Even when they were in the same room, the distance between them remained the breadth of an ocean.

A woman with a plan

Over the years, Lili and I filled in the blanks as to how Auntie Astrid came to marry her Italian. It was important for us to know those things, after all. We were always ferreting out the family gossip, or gossip of any kind, really. With so many secrets, our need to know was insatiable. Growing up with Lili, I learnt that knowledge is currency – and how I gathered and hoarded every tantalising morsel!

When she was twenty-four years old, Auntie Astrid decided that South Africa did not hold good marriage prospects for her. It was whispered that she fell in love with her white boss, who would not marry her: it would mean they would have to leave the country, or she would have to be reclassified. Our grandmother would not entertain the humiliation involved in that process. Anyway, she reasoned, if he loved Astrid so much, he would be prepared to leave everything behind without hesitation.

But he too had a family and a mother with opinions. They persuaded him that the auto repair shop that he had inherited was too lucrative to give up for a woman, and that it demanded all his loyalty. Our mother told us bitterly one day that his family probably paid Astrid off – or maybe, in a rush of guilt, he paid her himself. That was her ticket to Canada.

Never again would she be on the losing end of love, Astrid decided. And never again would she return to these shores, where even love was legislated. She had a plan: a rich husband would compensate for her broken heart. So she set out to find him. Her plan was pretty straight-forward. All she had to do was hang out in the right places; her looks would do the rest.

As soon as she arrived in Toronto, she located the most expensive hotel and stayed there until her money ran out. But there weren't that many takers – most men seemed to travel with their wives. Soon she had to resort to plan B. Who were the men who earned the money in the city of Toronto? Aha! A doctor would do. So she applied for cleri-cal work at the biggest hospital, and that is where she met her Italian. They married with due haste as, in the tradition of my family, my cousin Ricardo was on the way.

Something for the pain

Astrid sits with me, next to my mother.

"Ah May," she cries, "all this time, and now this!" It is obvious that she is heartbroken. "Is there really no hope?" she asks me in despair.

I look at her, but I cannot find the words, cannot even utter a simple word like "yes".

She sees the answer on my face. "You're a really brave girl, Danika."

"Sometimes I wish I didn't have to be so brave," I say, surprising myself with my sincerity. I leave it hanging. Astrid has no reply to this.

"I wish Ma was here," I say suddenly. "She would know what to do."

Astrid nods weakly and then buries her face in her hands.

Ma believed that for whatever ailed you, there was an old Dutch remedy – easily procured from the corner shop or local supermarket. Anything from a cold to a major disease. If you had a sore stomach, there was Jamaica Ginger, and Borsdruppels mixed with honey could cure any cough. She wasn't one for doctors or hospitals.

"My mother couldn't afford to take me or my brothers and sisters to the doctor every time we got sick," she'd explain whenever the topic arose. "And look how healthy I am!"

Later in her life, Ma learnt about the health benefits of herbs. When I visited her for lunch, she'd cut up garlic cloves and nasturtium leaves to put on her bread and cheese. It annoyed me – and it annoyed her that I refused to try any of it.

That was Ma. How I miss her, with her no-nonsense approach to life. She would have known what to do.

Good life

I think about how my mother could find beauty in death. After Ma died, she told everyone how peaceful the passing was. There was no infirmity, no lingering. No pain that we knew of. She went "peacefully in her sleep", as the saying goes. In her own bed, her own house.

"Ma had a good life," I told my mother at the time.

"Yes," my mother agreed; then wryly, "It's a pity she never got to read all those newspapers."

Despite how sad we were at the time, the two of us burst out laughing. For years and years – at least as long as I could remember – Ma had been collecting interesting newspaper articles that she wanted to get around to reading one day. They were stacked in dusty, yellowing piles in her bedroom. We would all comment how it was a fire hazard or how it would attract vermin, but she refused to get rid of them. By the time she died, some of those piles reached the ceiling. I know. I had to help my mother clear them away.

Ma died a few years back, but she had had a good life. She was content. I remember how proud she was when the new government came in. With her rickety legs, she went along to vote – all of us together. The tears streamed down her face as she told everyone who would listen how long she had waited for this day. She reminded us how she refused to vote in the tricameral or "puppet" parliament elections of 1984. She never forgot any of the indignities she was made to suffer under the old government, and would not let us forget either. I'm glad she lived to see that.

She also got to see Astrid return to South Africa, although the tall

Canadian flag proudly displayed in Astrid's front yard incensed her. Still, she was proud of her grandchildren. Yes, she had had a good life.

When Astrid moved back to South Africa after her divorce, her children stayed behind in Canada. South Africa, after all, is for the brave. My cousins couldn't understand how I could choose to remain here when I didn't have to, but I suppose that I am my mother's child. South Africa is in my blood.

Winter 1985

Of course, my father finds another job. Eventually. He is adamant about one thing: he will no longer work away from home. Look how things turned out when he did that. At least now he can keep an eye on things! The only job he can find is as a mechanic and the pay is much less than he was earning before, but at least his work is nearby. He can come home for lunch.

Every night, he comes home tired and complaining about how hard he works. As soon as he walks in, he collapses on the couch and calls me to take off his shoes and socks. I wonder why he can't take them off himself like we all do, but my mother says it is his culture. His father was the same, she says. I do it, grudgingly. His boots are dirty and covered in grease from the cars he works on, but things are better in the house when we do what our father says. Because when he is not complaining about work, our father finds other things to complain about. The dirty house, the food, the noise that Lili and I make and, of course, how lucky we all are. The only thing that makes him madder is the way the darkies are going on in the townships.

My father has new friends now, from his work. Sometimes he doesn't come home straight away. He and his friends go out for a drink. My mother says they must be drinking in the workshop, because where else can they go, all dirty? We say nothing; we're just glad for the respite, to be able to eat our supper in peace without worrying whether our elbows are on the table or if grace was said.

I wish that my father still worked away, but obviously I would never tell him that. I still want him to see me. To see that even if I'm not a boy, I am still good enough. I show him my report cards, expecting the praise that Ma and my mother heap on me, but he says that he is busy; that he'll look at it later. He never does. Doesn't he like me any more?

But every now and then, it's almost like old times. Like when our father takes me and Lili with him to visit Auntie Jill. He takes a bottle of whisky, and he and Auntie Jill drink it in her bedroom with the door closed.

We have to play outside with Auntie Jill's children, Pam and Louise, even though it's cold. They are much older than us and grumble at their mother. Auntie Jill is nice and gives us sweets. Later, when we're in the car to go home, our father tells us that we mustn't tell our mother where we were. She doesn't like Auntie Jill. I keep the secret, but I am not sure whether Lili does.

But it doesn't need me or Lili to say anything; it seems that our parents fight every day now. Over what, I don't know. In the mornings when we wake up and get dressed, we hear their muffled voices in the kitchen over the steaming whistle of the kettle. As soon as Lili or I walk in, it's all smiles and, "Hurry up and eat your breakfast, you'll be late for school."

♠

There are many whispers going around the playground. Opposite our school is a high school. Sometimes, during break, we can see the police vans and trucks parked outside. Sometimes a helicopter flies overhead making a loud whirling noise and all of us look out of the high windows, trying to catch a glimpse of it. Our teacher looks at her watch, clicks her teeth and tells us to pay attention. But it is difficult to pay attention when there are so many exciting things going on outside.

We have our own ideas about what is happening, but no one is quite sure. The grown-ups don't tell us anything. Exasperated, I ask Lili what it's about, and she tells me her teacher says the high-school children are protesting.

"Protesting against what?" I demand, but Lili just says, "Things."

When I tell my mother about the police, she says I mustn't worry about such things; then she looks at me as if she is concentrating on something really hard. "Go and play at the back," she says.

I'm about to remind her that it's getting dark and it's very cold out, but think better of it.

"Danny, will you please tell Lili that I want to see her," my mother says crisply.

My hand is on the back door; I am about to go out. "Is Lili in trouble?" I ask hopefully.

My mother pretends she has not heard me.

♠

Then there are other matters to occupy our attention. Once we make things more comfortable at home, treading around our father's moods, it isn't long before he starts to find fault with his boss.

Our mother says, "What will ever satisfy you? Being your own boss?"

Our father ignores her. This is one of his favourite tricks. He ignores us when he doesn't want to answer our questions.

His bad mood can last all evening. Sometimes he'll look at the plate of food set before him on the table and push it away. "What's this rubbish?" he'll say. "Stew again? Why can't you do anything right?"

Lili and I will try to get up from the table, but he'll push us back into our seats. "You girls don't leave the table until you've finished everything on your plates, do you hear me?" It is never a question. Then our mother has to fry him a steak or chops. Stew, it seems, is only good enough for women and children.

No matter how much our feelings are hurt, we learn to say nothing. Our mother's rebellions are limited by her impotence: she is financially dependent on him. One day Lili says to her, "Why don't you get a job, Mommy? Then you won't have to put up with all that."

Our mother explains again that she did not finish school before Lili came along and that she is not qualified for anything. Anyway, mothers don't work – unless there's no father.

Still, our mother enrols at a correspondence college to complete her matric. This is another secret. She hides her books in our bedroom among our schoolbooks, and all her letters are sent to Ma's house.

Life goes on. Even if we are not happy, what is most important is that we appear to be.

♠

Our mother's screams break up our play outside, as we try to make the most of the scant sunshine. The noise is coming from her bedroom. Lili and I rush to see what is wrong. I get to the door first; turn the knob. It is latched from the inside. I can hear my father's raging. My mother has gone silent, just heaving gasps of air. The sound of terror and tears.

I'm so small, I don't need to crouch to see through the keyhole. Right in front of me, in my direct line of sight, our mother is kneeling on the floor. Our father stands in front of her with his belt raised. His belt! The same belt he is always threatening us with! I always thought it was just that, a threat. Our mother begs him to stop. My and Lili's shouts and pleas join with hers, but our father doesn't stop. Or he doesn't hear us. After a few minutes, Lili runs to our room and slams the door. But I keep watch.

Why did I have to see it? The room is big; why fight in front of the door? Or was my mother trying to get away? The door never opens and eventually I fall asleep on the floor outside.

I wake up early. The wooden floor is uncomfortable and cold. Lili must have put my blanket over me, since the bedroom door is still locked from the inside. She makes me breakfast and we sit at the kitchen table eating our toast. When my father comes in, I stare hard at the cracked yellow Formica of the table.

Even though I know it will get me into trouble, I tear away pieces of the Formica where it has come loose. He says nothing; hums a tune as he puts water in the kettle. After his coffee, he goes to work like normal. Lili and I go to school and pretend that nothing is wrong. Our mother spends the day in bed.

♠

It is supper time. I am nervously struggling with the unruly peas on my plate. The braised liver is disgusting – it has never been a favourite of mine. The fat on the fried onions that my mother always makes with liver is cooling and congealing, forming little crystals. We are eating supper as a family. Our father confidently asks his Lord to bless our food and we all mumble our amens, but things are not the same. I don't think they will ever be.

No one says a word; the silence is broken only by the soft, steady rain forming diamond drops on the window. This is what I concen-trate on: the patterns the rain makes as it hits the glass. For some rea-son, nobody has drawn the curtains.

My father coughs abruptly. We all flinch. He smiles ruefully at us. There is no hint of an apology. Just a look, as if we are the ones he finds lacking. We have not mentioned the other day. Not even separately. Maybe if you pretend that something never happened, then it didn't really.

My father clears his throat loudly, but this time we are prepared for it.

"I have something to say," he states tonelessly.

We look up. Maybe this is it. Maybe he's going to say that he's sorry and that it will never happen again. Maybe then we can forgive him.

Instead, he says, "That bloody crook at the garage let me go."

We look at him in confusion. This is not what we were expecting.

Sensing this, he explains in his most superior manner: "I lost my job. That bastard says he can't afford to keep me on."

Not again, I think.

My mother takes a deep breath and says blandly, "Yes, Trevor."

Pure

I go through the motions, trying to find comfort in the mundane. The ordinary things. I leave the hospital late at night. My flat is in darkness. The air smells stale, as no windows have been left open. Kick my boots off, but leave my socks on. My feet welcome the freedom. I pad down the carpeted passage to the kitchen. Damn, the light's fused. I must remember to buy globes tomorrow. The light from the fridge casts a menacing glow as I search for food. I am famished.

I don't eat at the hospital. There is something perverse about eating when next to me my mother is being fed some substance from a drip. Most of her veins have collapsed, so now they have connected the intravenous tube to one in her neck. Once I would have known the name of that vein – neatly coloured blue for veins and labelled in my biology book.

There is nothing to eat. All that was once edible is shrunken, dehydrated or rancid, including the well-meant food from friends. How I hate wasting food. "Waste not, want not" – that message had been drummed into my head. I find a packet of muesli in the cupboard, so old that it is soft. But I eat it anyway. Straight out of the packet, like chips. I consider pouring myself a drink, but know that once I start, I will not stop. I need to remain sober. I need to be alert and attuned in case that call comes. I may need to drive.

In the crashing silence, I run myself a bath. Smoke another cigarette as I wait for the water to fill the tub. My mouth is dry, so I drink some water from the tap. The pipes in the bathroom are loud and creak in anguish as the water spurts. I really should be more considerate of my neighbours, but right now, I cannot care.

The temperature hits me once I am standing in the bath. The water scalds my feet, which are cold and sore from being pinched into my boots all day. Funny the little things we do to comfort ourselves, like wearing boots for confidence.

"Mommy, why do you like your bath water so hot?" The water in which she is sitting burns my hands as I tentatively dip them in. I love the pine-scented smell of my mother's bath water. "Your skin is all angry and red, like chicken skin. Doesn't it burn you?"

"I like my water hot. That way, little girls can't climb into the bath with their mommy. Now go and see what your sister's doing."

I scrub the hospital smell from my body. That sickening smell that seeps through my pores and clings to my hair like cigarette smoke. I lie in the bath and let the water cover me. My hair straightens out around me, becomes caught under my arms. So much hair. I cannot get clean. I wash and rewash my hair – though I know that the "repeat" instruction on shampoo bottles is just a ploy to get us to use more. I exfoliate my legs and then shave. The long stream of dissipating blood from a nick on my leg fascinates me. I need to buy new razors.

I lie in the scummy filth until the water is cold. I am so tired. So tired, I don't worry about drying my hair. I get into bed dripping wet, still wrapped in my towel. Who cares about catching a cold?

Another day

I peer at my mother. There is no change. She has remained apparently stable for the past few days; the deterioration is subtle, gradual.

I discover that once you have visited the teeming, seething hospital often enough or for a long enough stretch of time, you can shut out the noise that surrounds you until you exist in your own cocoon of sound-lessness. Once I discover this, I need to break the silence. I start to fidget, root around in my bag for some gum, lip gloss – any distraction. I wish I had a magazine or book to read. A crossword to complete. I could go to the shop, but I don't have the energy or the inclination to drag my-self there. Waiting for the unreliable lifts, dodging the sick and the des-perate. No thank you. Anyway, the shop screams of germs. I avoid it as much as I can, succumbing only to the occasional bottle of water. ("No, thanks, I don't need a straw.")

My officious and stylish black leather Filofax is at the bottom of my bag. A relic of another time. It should provide a meagre distraction. I rifle through it, amazed at my two very different lives this year. Juxtaposed with work meetings, functions and the occasional date are the later doctor's appointments, the obscure medical terms that I would painstakingly write down to research later.

There are so many blank pages now. What is there to schedule or to record? I stare out of the window at the little patch of sky visible between the towering walls of this brick colossus.

I will capture my memories. Perhaps then I can make sense of them.

I have often listened in amazement when my friends recalled their idyllic childhood years or spoke about the relationships they enjoyed with both their parents. What would that be like? Would I be a different person?

I am often envious of the relative calmness of my friends' lives. Husbands, children, committees. I have no such ties. Soon I will lose another fragile bond. I am becoming resigned to this fact.

The weight of memory

I am sitting pensively, sucking on my pen, squinting to recall all the things that have happened before, when Astrid walks in. She is becoming a regular visitor, though not a predictable one.

Astrid and I make small talk, exchange pleasantries – we are on our best behaviour, in deference to my unaware mother. Not that my mother would be especially polite, I speculate, but we do what we think is appropriate. Impulsively, I decide to ask Astrid about the tension that existed between the two of them. She is more garrulous than my mother, and somehow easier to approach.

"How come you and my mother were not close?" I venture as we sit on either side of the woman in question.

Astrid looks at me in surprise, then furtively glances at my mother, as if to ascertain whether or not she can hear us. After an infinitesimal pause, she tries to answer my question, her twang softening as her voice is lowered.

"Oh the usual, my girl," she starts. "We allowed men to come between us. I never thought your father was good enough for my sister. Even before they were married, he used to treat her badly . . ." She stops suddenly, unsure whether to continue. Uncertain of how much I know.

"It's fine," I reassure her, "I remember."

"Well, your father wanted to make a punching bag of your mother. I stepped between them. That's when he tried to hit me. I'll never forget it! Pa was still alive and he did nothing, though he must have heard the commotion.

"I ran over to Mrs Carelse and we called the police. And do you know what? Your mother must have been in love with your father, because she lied for him. Told the police that I was making it all up. That he would never do such a thing, though you could see the red hand-marks on her face. The police could do nothing.

"When they left, I'll never forget the look your father gave me. So smug, so satisfied. I'm sorry to say this to you, my girl, but I always thought your mother could do better. He just wasn't our type."

As she talks, I feel the burden of my parents once more settling upon me. I cannot believe what my mother had put up with.

Winter 1985

A month passes and still our father is not back at work. Lili and I start to wonder if he is ever going back. We know this question burns within our mother the most.

The atmosphere in our house is heavy, yet delicate. Anything can ignite a spark. Simple things like answering back or leaving the dishes unwashed in the sink. The two of us complain. After all, it is our father who makes the mess. But we gripe to each other only. Our father is not someone you complain about to his face, even in a joke. And there are other, unknown currents at work in our house. I cannot put my finger on them. Still, they are there.

"I have found a job," our mother declares out of the blue. It is supper time and we are unenthusiastically eating our frikkadels, which taste more like bread than meat. For a brief moment, we stop eating.

Lili and I are excited and cannot hide it. Our father says nothing, only snorts. After all his dire warnings about his wife working, his reaction is surprisingly mute. He carries on eating. I push my mashed potato around my plate. The three of us are expectant. What will he do?

After a while he says, "Well, what do you want? A bloody award?"

He gets up abruptly, leaves his chair out and turns the TV on. Loud. I address my mashed potato with renewed determination.

Lili and I watch in amusement as our mother gets ready for work. She is so nervous, but more than that, there's the excitement. The glow and sparkle in her eyes. As we stare at her outfits, we don't care if we are late for school. Her pleasure is infectious. The three of us are almost delirious. This is such an occasion: our mother's first day at work. She has never worked before in her life. She's been lucky and managed to get an office job. She is what is known as a debtor's clerk. She explains that this means she must make sure that people who owe her company money pay their debts. The company is a big clothing factory and her boss is called Mr Abraham.

Our mother tells us that she is very fortunate to get this job – and without any experience! She says that not so long ago, the only jobs open to women like her were as nurses and teachers. Or in a factory, but in the actual factory, making things. Not in the office. That's not so bad, she says. In Ma's day, women could work "in service" only, which means as a maid. My father's two eldest sisters work in factories too, they are machinists. Luckily, it's not the same factory as my mother's. That would be embarrassing, she says.

Eventually she decides on a beautiful purple dress. Purple is my mother's favourite colour. This dress has matching purple shoes. My mother likes things to match. She wears her big purple and yellow plastic bangles and bright yellow earrings. We watch wide-eyed as she rims her eyes with black kohl and paints on a bright pink smile. We are suitably impressed: she looks so fashionable. Her hair is shiny, almost liquid. Then she sprays on her favourite perfume, Youth Dew, and she's ready. She bends to kiss us goodbye, then grimaces. "I don't want to smudge my lipstick," she explains as she hugs us instead. "Be good and wish me luck," she says. "Your father will take you to school."

Then she clops out on her high heels, like a little girl wearing her mother's shoes.

♠

Our mother does not have many friends. It's not so strange that you'd notice, but she doesn't seem to enjoy the company of other women. She has many male friends, though. They are all in love with her, she tells Lili and myself conspiratorially.

We are her confidantes. She cries as she tells us how unhappy she is in her marriage. I fetch the tissues and get her a glass of water as her tears come out in great gulps. Lili strokes her hand, offering her the only comfort she knows. Lili is twelve and I am seven, yet we feel very grown-up.

We tell her that she must leave our father. That we won't mind, we won't miss him. But she looks at us – deeply, sincerely, tearfully – and says, "You children are the only reason I stay with him."

Making our mother happy becomes our mission. The two of us decide that we can't let our mother come home from a hard day's work to a dirty house, so every afternoon we rush home from school and clean. Now that my mother is working, my father makes no effort to find work of his own, but according to him, cleaning is a woman's job. Most days, we come home to find him lying on the couch in his underpants.

At first, I try to humour him into helping us. I try to get him to make supper by flattering him. Usually, he ignores my patter. He pretends to be asleep. We learn to clean around him; we learn to cook, after a fashion. My one rebellion is to refuse to touch his hard, crusty socks, which he leaves wherever he takes them off.

Sometimes we come home from school and his friends are there. When he hears us come in, our father will start loudly complaining about how dirty the house is and how there's never any cooked food. The men drink their whisky, play their cards, exchange tips for the horses and talk their big talk about their big wins. From these afternoons, I learn that men never mention their losses.

My father can be very friendly towards us at such times. He'll call us in to greet his friends. But only I will go into the lounge. Lili walks straight to our room. She is still not speaking to him. He will kiss me hello and ask me about school. Later, he will say to me, "Go make us some sandwiches, my girl."

And although I am glad that my father is being pleasant, I know that later, when my mother comes home from work, the drama will start. She will complain about the mess and the drunken friends and my father will shout that this is his house. Lili and I do our best to tidy his mess before our mother comes home. We collect the dirty glasses, empty ashtrays, make ourselves indispensable.

There are days when we come home from school and our father is not there. My mother gives Lili a key to the back door so we can let ourselves in. My class finishes before Lili's. I now walk home from school by myself. Or at least, a bunch of us who live in the same area walk home together, usually with someone's mother. I am glad that they don't turn up our road, because sometimes, if my father is not home, I have to sit on the stoep and wait for Lili to come home. Sometimes Auntie Ruthie calls me over to have some cooldrink with her, but she only buys powdered Kool-Aid, which I do not like. Auntie Ruthie asks me all sorts of questions when we are alone. When I tell my mother about them, it makes her cross; so the next time Auntie Ruthie calls me over, I politely tell her, "No thank you."

Once in a while, we come in to find our father passed out on the couch, the open bottle of whisky next to him. Water pooling in the ice bucket with all the different flags on it. A sticky glass. On those days, we know better than to complain about the mess, or to try to cajole him into helping us. His whisky breath is as foul as his mood. We keep his secret, hiding the bottle before our mother comes home. Anything to avoid hearing the inevitable argument about how he is spending money we do not have on his drinking.

Other times, my father comes home only when we are sleeping. On these nights, we all have disturbed sleep. When he returns from wher-ever he goes, he makes so much noise that we all wake up. Swearing at imaginary obstacles that trip him up. "Can't even keep the house clean," he mutters under his breath, but muttering is not his style; the accusa-tion booms and reverberates throughout the house.

Who can't keep the house clean, I think to myself – but I know that it is all of us who are to blame. As he thunders to his bedroom, I flinch. "Please say nothing," I whisper, as if my mother can hear me. Tonight I want to sleep. Let him pass out and fall asleep. Then we can all sleep. My mother says that it's when he is half drunk that he is at his worst. I hope that he is properly drunk.

♠

The day our mother receives her first pay cheque, the three of us cele-brate. She is so proud, she brings the cheque home to show me and Lili before banking it.

"You girls must make sure that you always have your own money," she tells us solemnly. "Then no man can think that he owns you. Don't forget: there is no better freedom than earning your own money."

The two of us nod our heads. We know what our mother means.

She says to us dreamily, "My girls will get an education and never have to rely on a man for anything."

The Saturday after payday, before the bills are paid and groceries bought, our mother takes Lili and me clothes-shopping in Town. She doesn't like driving in Town, so we take the train. We have so much fun, trying on the latest fashions at the station market and walking around the Golden Acre. The Golden Acre is gigantic, but I don't feel tired from all the walking. Afterwards, we have fish and chips for lunch, but the best part is the bright-pink rose-syrup milkshake that we have on the Parade before we board the train for home.

♠

The teachers know that something is wrong, though there is no one I can talk to. They comment on the state of my hair and my uniform, exchanging knowing, pointed looks that say it all. I am a child. I dare not look back at them with defiance in my eyes, meeting their stares. Instead, I look down at my black school shoes and agree that they need polishing.

"How could your mother let you leave the house looking like this?" They question me with eager, glinting eyes.

I say nothing. I look down at the scuffed school shoes that my father used to polish for me, a long time ago. I pray for it to end. Pray that soon they will pick on someone else. I can't very well say that my hair looks untidy because I brushed it myself this morning. Or that my uniform looks a mess because it's my job to wash it with Sunlight soap every Friday after school, and that maybe the stains can't come out – I should know better than to eat in it or sometimes cook in it after school. I cannot tell them that my mother is always too busy to iron the dress, although I leave it in the lounge anyway, hoping that she'll see it when she irons her skirts and blouses for work. I do it myself – often on a Monday morning, when I am already late for school. I don't say that my mother often doesn't know how I look in the morning when I go to school, because she has already left for work, catching a bus and a train to make it on time since my father says that he needs the car.

I cannot say these things because this is not the way things are done. The other mothers at my school are the kind who bake cakes and sew hems and help their children with their needlework projects. They are older than my mother and do not wear shorts and miniskirts or smoke cigarettes. They do not cry in front of their children for no reason or worry about paying bills and the electricity getting cut. No, these things I must keep to myself.

♠

Now that our mother is working, we have to get up extra early to be done in time. We cannot rely on our father to take us to school. If we are not ready by the time our mother has to leave, then we have to walk to school by ourselves. I like to walk with her to the bus stop, which is on the way to school. Her high heels clipsing along as I struggle to keep up with her. But my mother is always in a rush, so that seldom happens. Lili is supposed to walk with me now, though she always runs off ahead, complaining that I make her late.

One day I am late for school. Boomer follows me and I have to take him back home. The bell will ring any minute and I am still a few roads away – I will have to run all the way. The more I think of the trouble I'll be in if I am not on time, the more difficult it becomes to breathe. I gulp in air, but the air is trapped in my lungs, pooling in my throat. I cannot breathe. Panicking, I start gasping for breath. I can hear my heart pumping loudly, but still I cannot breathe. I feel like I am going to faint.

An old lady watering her garden sees me and calls me over. I know that I am not supposed to speak to strangers and that I am very late, but the lady seems so kind. She leaves the hose running in the garden and walks over to me.

"Coo-ee," she says, "are you okay?"

"I'm late for school," I reply, in heaves and bursts.

"Where's your mother, my girl?" the lady asks me.

"She's gone to work," I explain, "and I was too late to go with her. Now I'm late for school and I'll get a hiding!" I sob.

"Come inside, my girl, I'll get you some sugar water," the lady says.

I follow hesitantly, standing just outside the gate as she closes the tap.

"Come on, I won't bite!" she insists with a gentle smile.

Her smile reassures me and I follow her to her kitchen, disobeying all the warnings about not going into strange people's houses. The house smells familiar and inviting. Like lavender polish and bread baking. It smells of an old lady's house. Just like Ma's.

The lady gives me a glass of sugar water and offers me some sweets from a jar. "Take some with you," she insists. "There's only me to eat the sweets. I have a granddaughter your age, but I don't see her. She lives in Australia with her parents now."

I nod wisely at the kind lady. "We have cousins in Canada," I offer.

"Are you feeling better?" she asks.

"Yes," I reply softly, studying my fingernails.

"Good," she says. "Come on, I'll walk you to school."

As we walk, the lady tells me, "You shouldn't be walking alone, my girl. Bad things are happening in our country these days."

She takes me right to my class and speaks to my teacher, who curtly directs me to my desk. The others in the class look at me curiously. We all wait for Miss Daniels to scold me for being late, but she carries on with the lesson once the lady is gone.

During interval, my friends ask me who the lady was.

"My grandmother," I reply.

♠

Lili says to my mother, "Did you hear that the government made a new homeland? It's called the State of Emergency."

"Where did you hear that, Lili?" my mother asks sharply, spoiling Lili's joke.

"I don't know," Lili mumbles.

"What is the State of Emergency?" I ask my mother.

Frowning, she looks at me. Then, glancing around her before she speaks, she says, "It's just the government's nonsense, my girl. It's not here, only in certain parts of the country – so don't worry about it."

Her answer doesn't satisfy me, but I know better than to press her.

Just as we are about to eat supper, the phone rings. My mother looks at the phone grimly, her lips pursed. "Ignore it," she says.

"No," my father insists, "it might be important." He makes no effort to answer.

The phone rings again and we wait in suspense.

"Danika, go answer the phone," my father tells me. "Take a message if it's for me. I'll phone back later."

"Hello?" I say tentatively into the phone.

"Danika Matthews? Is that you?"

"Yes, Miss Daniels," I respond, recognising her clipped tones.

"May I speak with your mother, please?"

"Yes, Miss Daniels." In my nervousness, my voice falters slightly. "One second."

"Mommy," I say unnecessarily, "my teacher's on the phone."

I am trembling as I hand over the phone; trembling as I resume my seat at the table. Unexpectedly, Lili smiles at me weakly, in brave solidarity. My father is not that kind. He glares at me. Supper is getting cold and it is all my fault.

"What the blazes is this about?" he demands. "What have you got up to now?"

I shrug, not meeting his eyes. But I know. They talk for an eternity – or at least, Miss Daniels talks and my mother listens, occasionally answering "Yes" or "No" or "I understand."

"Yes, Miss Daniels. Thank you." My mother replaces the telephone receiver, then reconsiders, leaving it off the hook.

"So?" my father barks. "What was that about?"

"Nothing important," my mother replies evasively. "Just some meeting."

Having said grace before the call, we pick up our knives and forks and start eating our tomato bredie and rice.

♠

We are aware that bad things are happening in our country every day. The word for bad things is "unrest". Every night we watch the TV news, desperate for a respite. PW Botha comes on almost every night, wagging his finger at us in admonition. Railing against those who want to see the downfall of this land. His prominent head reminds me of a hard-boiled egg before you crack the shell.

My mother tells Lili and me excitedly, "It won't be long . . . the Russians are coming!"

"What will the Russians do?" I ask. This is interesting.

"Save us," my mother replies.

I savour this information, trying to make sense of it. Then I ask, "What colour are the Russians, Mommy?" It is an obvious question: the colour of our saviours.

My mother looks at me curiously, then thinks. "Red," she replies after a long pause.

I roll back the sleeves of my cardigan and look at my arms in curiosity, eager to see the colour of my skin. It is a bit reddish. "Are we red? I think that I am a red person."

My mother looks at me and a rare smile brightens her face. "You're a funny girl, Danny," she laughs.

Just then my father walks into the room. I wonder how much he has heard, since he is clearly angry. "Stop putting ideas into Danika's head, May," he says.

"Trevor, you must stop burying your head in the sand," my mother replies, uncharacteristically firm.

My father belches and walks out.

♠

We can't believe our luck, having such a long interval. It's almost like the bell that calls us back to our classrooms forgot to ring. Some of us who wear watches start making our way back anyway. After every break, we have to line up in the quad outside our classrooms before we go back inside. But the bell doesn't ring and the teachers don't come out of the staff room. It is like they forgot about us.

The strangeness of this starts all kinds of stories. We're going to go home early. Or perhaps today is a special day, only nobody told us. Maybe it's got something to do with the police trucks and vans that are parked outside the high school opposite. But they've been there for a while; there is nothing new about their presence.

We have heard stories about the bigger children staying away from school. The word "boycott" has started to come up in conversations, although we are not totally sure what it means. I am soon bored with playing endless hopscotch games, so I make my way to Lili's side of the school. She will know what's going on.

"Where's Lili?" I ask one of the spotty boys in her class, my hands on my hips.

The boys in her class are so immature, Lili says. She loves explaining things to me that make her seem so important in my eyes. Like how boys' voices can break. That is why they have so many pimples. I don't see the connection, but don't question her.

The boy with the broken voice and the pimply face points to the lawn. Lili is sitting in a circle with her friends, including the unfortunate Monique. Undeterred, I walk over to her.

"What's happening?" I ask.

"Danny, why aren't you in your class?" Lili accuses. "And why do you look so untidy?"

Lili is never one to miss an opportunity.

"I thought you would know what's happening," I say.

It is the right answer. Lili visibly puffs up with self-importance. "The teachers are having a meeting," she says, gesturing in the general direction of the staff room.

"What about?" I ask.

"I don't know," Lili admits. "Go back to your classroom, the bell will ring soon."

Eventually the bell rings. We line up by our desks expectantly, but Miss Daniels doesn't tell us to sit.

"Here's a letter to give to your parents tonight," she tells us. "Pack your bags and go home quickly. The school is closed. Those of you who have to wait for lifts can wait, but the rest of you must leave."

It must be another stay-away. We've had a few of these in the past month, but I don't know why.

The bell rings, signalling the end of school, before Miss Daniels finishes speaking.

Appearances are everything

Looking at my mother in the quiet of her hospital room, I allow my mind to wander. I look at her and think, what if she can see me? I imagine her assessing me critically. My hair, my nails, my clothes. My eyes, puffy and ringed. The conversations we had so many times come back to me: "You should always wear red," she'd advise me, "it suits your colouring." Or: "Why don't you girls look after your nails?" Astrid's visit has not helped, making me realise how much I have let myself go.

My mother's preoccupation with her looks came in later years. Before, when Lili and I were younger, it was we who were concerned about her clothes. For a considerable time after she lost the baby, she wore the same green velour tracksuit every day. It looked like she never changed out of it. It was the muddiest green colour with red piping, and it had shiny patches where the velour had been rubbed thin. Lili and I thought it was the ugliest thing. I think this was the first time that we noticed the depth of our mother's unhappiness.

Eventually, Lili summoned the courage to confront my mother about the tracksuit. It had to go! My mother must have been shocked by this young girl telling her that she needed to change. That night, she ran herself a hot bubble bath and took off the dreaded tracksuit. She never wore it again. Later it was cut up and became polish rags. But even more amazing, the next day, my mother went to the hairdresser. By the time Lili and I came home from school her long, wavy hair had been transformed into a short, glossy bob.

She looked like a different person. I missed playing with her long hair. When she was in a good mood, she would allow me to brush it and I'd twist the hair around the brush to make curls. Her hair curled so easily, unlike mine, which had to be put in scratchy plastic rollers if I wanted the slightest curl. And if I shook my hair too vigorously, the curl would simply fall out and my hair would be straight once more.

When I get home, I call my hairdresser on her cellphone. Usually I would never impose on anyone that late, but I need her help. Would she be able to squeeze me in the next morning? We make the usual small talk and then I ring off. She knows about my mother, I think, from the solicitous tone of her voice. It is not unlikely. Cape Town is a small place and I have referred some of my friends to her. Perhaps one of them said something.

The next morning, I have the works: my hair is cut and coloured the brightest red. I relax completely under the strong fingers of the shampooist. Revel in the warm spray of the water. I can let my hair look bright, even though I feel anything but. My hair is the greatest barometer of my mood. I think that if my hair looks good, then I am good. Forget the self-help books, I say, just get a new hairstyle.

As I walk out into the bright day, certain that the sunlight is catching the subtleties of my new hair colour, I feel guilty. As if my pleasure in my brilliant hairdo is perverse.

Nothing else matters

Buoyed by my new hair colour, I decide to make an appearance at work. Maybe I can persuade Alison to go to lunch. I promise myself that I will be away from the hospital for a short while only.

The atmosphere is changed as soon as I walk into reception.

"Hi." I greet Gavin, the firm's politically correct receptionist, with a brightness I do not feel. I am tense. I have been away from work for two months. Far too long.

Gavin looks at me in surprise. "Are you back now?" he asks, unsure if condolences are in order.

"No," I reply, "just visiting."

"Oh!" he says, embarrassed. Then, remembering his tact, "How's your mother?"

"The same."

Gavin looks stricken as I make my way to the open-plan office. I immediately see the reason for his consternation. My desk is occupied. I walk over to Alison.

"Hi," I say, "how's it going?"

Everyone's eyes are on me. Alison jumps up when she sees me.

"Oh, Danny, this is Zani," she says meaningfully. "She's helping out until you come back."

I smile sincerely. I am in no way threatened or put out. I understand about workloads, and though no one told me that they would be placing someone else in my job, it is not unexpected. I will deal with whatever happens when it happens.

"Nice to meet you," I say to Zani, who is clearly uncomfortable. It is obvious that she has heard all about me. "Do you want to go for lunch, Alison?" I suggest casually. "I was in the neighbourhood. I thought I'd see if you were free."

Alison and I go to lunch at a posh new restaurant overlooking the trendy Camps Bay beachfront. For the time we are there, I forget my mother and my anxiety about her. I allow myself to relax into the plush brown seats and wistfully stare out at the sea. By tacit agreement, we do not speak about my mother and what I am going through. Instead, we talk about men and relationships and work. I am uncharacteristically candid, although I have no new stories to add.

Recklessly, we finish a bottle of merlot, though she has to go back to work and I have to make an appearance at the hospital. Alison raises her eyebrows as I light up a cigarette, but says nothing. For a moment, things are back to how they used to be. For this short time, I can think only of myself. The hospital is a world away.

Nautilus

When I finally reach the hospital, I cannot help but feel guilty as I walk unsteadily to the room. My joy in my new hairdo dissipates as I wonder what the nurses must think.

Looking at her, I realise that every day my mother's condition becomes fractionally worse. I have learnt that any slight improvement is a false hope. Sometimes I talk to her and she seems to understand. I swear she does. Other times, I am here but it seems that she is elsewhere. Her body is a fragile shell, paper thin. Papery, yes – her skin rough and papery from not going outside. She is drying up from the outside in. Or is it the inside out? I rub lotions on her parchment skin. This one for the smell, that for the moisturising effects, others for their anti-bacterial qualities.

Am I holding her back? Am I keeping her from finding peace? There is so much I want to ask her. So much I need to know.

Be careful what you wish for

My mother and I had discussed euthanasia. Years ago, when I was a girl. I had done an oral project on the subject. Of course it was my mother's suggestion. What do young kids know about such a serious subject? I remember that there was a big media debate about euthanasia at the time.

My mother explained the concept to me. Together, we discussed whether it was right or wrong. The life of a child is one of absolutes; there are no in-betweens. As I formulated my stance, my mother convinced me of the validity of her point of view: of course it was right!

I know that soon I will have to let go, but theorising and postulating is so much easier when you do not have to make a real-life decision.

We were always discussing her death. Long, long before there was even a hint of this illness. How much my mother would hate this.

"I want to go quickly," she'd say. "I don't want to be a burden to anybody."

"How could you ever be a burden, Mom?" I'd ask.

Over the road from us was a house of old ladies. Or at least, Mrs September was old; her daughter, Miss Monica, merely seemed so. Miss Monica was what was impolitely referred to as an "old maid". Mrs September was already old when we moved in. But nice old. When we visited her, she'd give Lili and me stale Marie biscuits, which she kept hidden under her pillow where no one would find them. She kept a jar of sweets in the kitchen – for us only, it seemed, as it was never empty.

When she grew older, Mrs September became like a petulant child. If it had been anyone else, Lili and I would have made fun of her, but she was a special old lady and once she had given us biscuits and sweets. When we grew up and moved away, my mother, who was less kind, kept us updated on her antics. Eventually, she had to be tied to her bed to keep her under control.

I remember my mother's voice as she told me about it. Her shudder was audible over the line as she firmly said, "I never want to be that old."

The doctors have made it quite clear that they can increase her morphine dosage to bring about her "peace" sooner. Everything they say is veiled in euphemisms: it can be "any day now", or she can "linger". I know what they are hinting at. What they want me to consider.

Rationally, I can accept that it would indeed be peace. I can see that my mother's condition deteriorates with each day that she labours to draw breath, yet I think about the old maxim, "Where there is life there is hope." Who am I, or the doctors, to decide that her time is up?

So now I search the Internet for hope where once I searched to understand. I want to find that story of someone who survived this. Someone to tell me that everything I see, and ultimately know, is wrong. That she will get better. That I will be okay.

Spring 1985

We are relieved when spring comes. We always are – it's something we look forward to every year. Winter is too long and cold. Especially this winter. Yet this winter blazed to a fiery close. Spring is a time of new beginnings. Everyone knows that.

Every year on the day of the spring equinox, our school celebrates Spring Day. The children gather flowers that they've picked, from their own gardens or someone else's, and bring them to school, the little bunches wrapped in wet newspaper.

I love to pick the delicate snowdrops that grow wild in the field that we pass on the way to school. In class, all the flowers are jumbled together. We make little posies and buttonholes. Every teacher gets a posy of her own. The rest are distributed to the people at the old-age home nearby. Pupils who have been good are chosen to deliver the flowers personally. It is a time of celebration and hope.

This year, there will be no Spring Day festivities, since our school has been closed.

My father agrees that it is the right thing for the government to do – look at how they're killing one another in the townships. Look at the schoolchildren; they have no business rioting and disrupting things. And all the stay-aways! They are lazy, that's what. They don't want to go to school. They burn their books and their desks. My mother looks at him, her eyes narrowed and her nose ever so slightly flared, but all she says is that it was the government that closed the schools – my father doesn't know what he is talking about. My father says she's one to talk, what does she know anyway? He stresses that no wife of his is going to get involved in politics.

The day that we were sent home from school, our mother went to attend a meeting at the church in the next road from our house. Our father was so cross about it. He refused to go with her, but she went anyway. Lili went with her instead. That is how I know what happened.

They met in the church hall, the people from the neighbourhood meeting under cover of darkness. It was pitch, pitch dark. They had to be very careful, our mother told Lili, because the government had passed a law that made it illegal for more than two people to gather at a time. It was called an "illegal gathering". And you could go to jail for it. It was called "detention without trial".

I think that is why my father did not want my mother to go. Let alone Lili. But Lili doesn't listen to him. I wished that I was old enough to go too. It irritates me that Lili has the power to tell me or not to tell me what is going on. I have my ways too, but it's not that easy to hide in corners and listen to conversations these days. People have started to look around them before they talk to one another. And when they do, they stand close and talk softly.

Our school had been disrupted for days, but no more so than usual. The high school opposite started holding mass rallies. We could tell when these took place because of the Casspirs parked outside the school. Lili said that the high-school students were refusing to attend classes until the government withdrew the state of emergency. I asked her how she had become so smart all of a sudden. She shrugged and said that the children in her class with older brothers and sisters had told her.

Then one day my mother opened the newspapers and read that our schools were to be closed. Indefinitely. Officially. I had never seen her this angry before. She was so angry that she forgot about keeping us in the dark and shouted and swore about the government.

Now she is worried because Lili is supposed to start high school next year. How can children afford to lose their education? Our mother says it would be different if all the schools were closed, but it's only the coloured schools. She says that the government has no right to decide people's lives for them. What is going to happen to the children?

Our school was closed during the middle of exam time. Lili and I are happy for the long holiday. Or at least I think Lili is. She is worried about getting into high school and that she will have to repeat Standard Five. My mother tells Lili that it will never happen. Even if she has to work two jobs to send her to a private school next year.

I think that Lili is unhappy because she won't be able to see the boys in her class. She is becoming so big for her boots. She walks home from school with some of them. They stand on the corner, talking and laughing for ages. Talking about what, I don't know. As soon as she sees me, she tells me to buzz off and go home. The boys laugh and snicker at this as if it's the funniest thing. As if Lili is so cool. Don't worry, I always tell our mother. She says that Lili is becoming a teenager and that is how teenagers are. Moody and rude, I think, with lots of yellow pimples. I will get Lili back. Just wait and see!

The boys phone Lili at home. I used to answer the phone and pretend to be her – until she caught me. Now when the phone rings, she runs to answer it. I should tell my father. That will serve her right! Lili will be in a lot of trouble if he finds out.

Our father is not happy that he has to look after us during the day, now that the schools are closed and our mother is at work. Otherwise, I think he agrees with whatever the government says. He is always complaining about the people causing trouble in the townships. Lili and I are starting to hear snatches of what is going on. But not full stories. We try to make out what is happening from the little we hear.

Mainly what we hear are new words. Words like "Casspirs", "quirts", "hippos", "necklaces" . . . of course, this is not a normal kind of necklace. I hear the word at Ma's house for the first time. The word that somehow does not mean what I think it means. Ma and my mother are discussing serious business, because they are using that tone: soft, stilted, unfinished sentences. As soon as they see me, they stop talking. "What kind of necklace?" I want to know. Who got a new necklace? What are they talking about?

"Ag nothing," my mother says. "Who said anything about a necklace?"

I am not satisfied. I ask Lili about it, but she doesn't know either. Another intriguing phrase is "kangaroo courts". My father often rages against these after supper when he and my mother sit talking. It sounds like such a nice idea – kangaroos are nice; but I didn't know we had them here in South Africa. I thought they were found in Australia. I picture a kind of zoo, full of these cute animals that proudly carry their babies in pouches in front of them. When I ask my father about it, he says, "Stop being so big for your boots – go and help your sister in the kitchen."

When I tell Lili about it, she is curious too, and vows to help me get to the bottom of it. If she does find anything out, she doesn't tell me.

It is a secret that the day after the schools were closed, Lili and our mother went to school to march. They didn't tell me before they left. They pretended that she had to take Lili to the dentist. I am far too clever to willingly volunteer to go with them to the dentist. But a protest march is another thing!

Lili glows with excitement when she tells me what happened. First she makes me toss in – I have to swear that I won't tell our father. We know what he's like.

They left early, like leaving for school. I noticed this, but my mother said it was because she had to go to work after the dentist's appointment. There weren't that many parents, Lili said. Definitely under a hundred. Nor were all the teachers there. The school gates were locked, so they marched outside the gates, right around the school. Then the police came and told everyone they had to go home because they were not allowed to be there. They threatened to spray them with tear gas if they didn't disperse immediately.

"Weren't you scared?" I ask Lili.

She tosses her long brown ponytail and looks at me in amusement. "Don't be silly, Danny! It was the most exciting thing."

I can believe her. I wish I'd been there.

We hear our mother murmuring into the telephone. Someone is making her very angry, but she won't tell us who it is. Adults are very secretive. We walk into a room and conversation abruptly ends. We are told to play outside in the back. We are forbidden to play in the road. Although this is not new, now the rule is more forcibly applied.

♠

It is around this time that my mother starts painting again. In the open. My father says nothing. She starts attending the classes again. I don't think she needs them, because she is really good.

First she paints bowls of oranges and ordinary things like pencils, tables, flowers. Before long, she starts painting people from pictures in magazines and newspapers. She never asks me or Lili to pose for her.

I love the smell of my mother's paints; it reminds me of her. When she's at work and I miss her, I sniff the tubes of paint, being very careful to put them back exactly as I found them: we are not supposed to touch my mother's painting things. She buys Lili and me our own set of watercolours, but our pictures don't look like hers. I dip my fingers in the wet paint and make imprints of my fingers on the blank white paper.

When my mother is not painting her pictures, she is writing furiously in her notebooks.

"What you doing, Mommy?" I ask when I find her with her head buried in the black hard-cover books she prefers to write in. "What are you busy with?"

"Ag nothing," she answers as she slams the book closed. She must hide the books because I can't find them during the day when she's at work.

♠

Though winter is supposed to be over, the rain is endless. Our clothes remain unwashed as we wait for the weather to improve, forming mouldy mountains in the bathroom. At first we stamp it down in the washing basket, but when it overflows, Lili and I decide that we need to make a plan. For once, the mess doesn't seem to bother our father. Nor our mother, for that matter, although she makes sure that she has clean clothes for work.

Lili works out how to use the washing machine. We fill it to capacity. This full load hardly makes a dent in the dirty washing. Later, once the machine has stopped, we hang up the washing in the rain. We are so proud, we check and check that the washing is getting dry, though the rain only stops for a couple of hours at a time. I am trying to complete a puzzle when Lili calls me agitatedly, "Look, Danny, the washing is foaming."

I run outside to the line. It's the funniest sight, the suds streaming off the wet washing on the line.

"We must have forgotten to rinse out the soap powder," Lili explains seriously. She glares furiously at me as I laugh, so that I am immediately chastened. Still, it is the funniest thing!

Our mother tells us that we must stay inside the house when she's at work. When she leaves in the morning, she calls out to my sleeping father, "Trevor, keep an eye on the girls!" She tells us the government said that children are not allowed outside during the day. I think that this is a lie, since some children at other schools still go to school. Surely they can't stay inside all the time?

I must ask Tracey about this when she comes home. She's very upset that her school hasn't closed like ours has. Tracey's school is a private one, unaffected by the laws of our land.

"You're so lucky, Danny," she says. "It's so unfair."

But if I'm so lucky, why is my mother so upset that the schools are closed?

♠

Our mother is gone for at least an hour before our father gets up. Lili and I are cleaning the kitchen when he comes in and starts making his breakfast: a vienna-and-banana omelette. Disgusting. We can tell that he's in a good mood. He whistles as he cooks.

"You girls will be fine on your own today," he informs us. Then softer, more to himself than to us: "I got a hot tip for today."

Our father can never keep his news to himself.

"Who's –" I am about to ask him who will look after us, but Lili nudges me before I can finish my question.

"Get done, Danny," she says in her most bossy Lili voice. "I need place to pack."

Our father finishes his breakfast. He leaves his dirty dishes on the table. It's time for him to get ready. One thing about my father, he likes to look good. I glance at him as he comes out of the bedroom. He is wearing his favourite tweed jacket and a pair of jeans. Unfortunately, the look is marred by the bloody speck of toilet paper on his cheek. He must have nicked himself shaving, but we didn't hear him shout and swear like he usually does when this happens.

"Be good," he instructs Lili and me. "I'll be home before you know it."

The house smells of his aftershave when he leaves.

♠

As the heavy tanks come trundling down our road, we are drawn to our front windows, hiding away behind the lace curtains to see what is going on. They make such a noise. I can understand why they are called hippos. I know this, because Lili told me. She has taken to gleaning information from the newspapers, although this isn't easy – our mother hides most of the newspapers away once she's read them. Lili says the newspapers are not much help anyway.

Boomer starts to bark uncontrollably. It's a good thing he's inside the house. I run and put my arms around him to calm him and keep him quiet. Instinctively, I know that we don't want to attract any attention.

What is going on?

They have never come so close to our house before. I wonder what they want. Our area is usually quiet – our mother said so when Lili and

I asked her about any dangers we might face. We are far away from the action, she insisted. But now the action is coming to us!

We stay crouched behind the curtains, scarcely breathing in case the soldiers decide to come in. We have heard rumours of how they break down doors and burst into houses. We are so afraid that Lili doesn't mind when I grip her hand. Should we phone our mother, I ask in a whisper, but Lili says no, we shouldn't worry her at work. And in any case, we don't want anyone to hear us.

I grip Lili's hand tighter when the rumbling noise stops and we hear thuds, like when the birds drop green loquats on Ma's roof. Except it is much louder. Then we hear the shouts and the screams. We look at each other. What is this now?

I am so frightened that I wet myself. I only notice when Lili shouts at me. I am still holding her hand, standing in a puddle of my own pee. She flings her hand away from mine in disgust. "You big baby. Wait till I tell Mommy what you've done."

I am so frightened and ashamed that I cannot stop my wretched tears. Maybe I am a baby. The funny thing is, Lili runs me a bath and helps me clean up. And she doesn't tease me again that day.

My father has not returned by the time my mother comes home from work. I am so embarrassed that I make myself scarce. I will just die of shame if my mother finds out that I wet myself. I pray that Lili won't tell her.

"Where's your father?" I hear my mother asking Lili.

"He left," is Lili's reply. "I think he went to play the horses."

"Today?" our mother asks. Lili says nothing. It is quiet for a long time. I hear pots banging as our mother sees to supper. Then she asks, "What happened here today, Lili? Why are you so quiet, and where is you sister, for that matter?"

Then, uncharacteristically, Lili bursts into tears. Her sobs are so loud I can hear them from our room.

Lili must have told her the whole story, but my mother is not cross with me. She comes into my room and finds me lying on my bed.

"It's okay," she says, putting her arms around me, letting me cry.

Once we have calmed down, she goes to the front fence to find out what happened in our road. "Ruthie," she calls. It is at this fence that she and Auntie Ruthie have most of their conversations.

Auntie Ruthie comes out, wearing her apron. She must be eager to tell all – she's still busy drying her hands on a drying-up cloth. "Oh May," she says, flustered in her excitement. She clearly doesn't notice me and Lili standing at the front door, or maybe she doesn't care. "Such things we had here today!"

"What happened here?" my mother asks impatiently. "The girls said there was a Casspir in our road and some commotion. Do you know anything about it?"

Of course Auntie Ruthie knows all about it. She'd just been waiting for an opening. "Oh, you know those boys down the street, what's their surname, ah . . . Toefy – the Moslem family, you know? Well, my dear, the two youngest started throwing stones at the Casspir when it rode past. Luckily the police came and arrested them."

"But they're so young – why, they're just about the girls' ages," my mother says. "How could they be arrested?"

"It's the times we live in, May," Auntie Ruthie says wisely. "Children don't want to go to school, don't want to listen to their parents . . ."

"The government closed the schools, Ruthie," my mother reminds her sharply, turning away. "I must go and start my supper."

From the pulsing vein above her right eye, I can see that my mother is angry. We wait for an outburst, but she says nothing. She makes us eat our macaroni cheese, bath and go to bed early. We protest bitterly. After all, we don't have to go to school tomorrow, so why should we go to sleep so early?

Our mother looks at us intently, her eyes glinting in the weak light of the chandelier. Several of the globes need to be replaced. "I mean it, get to bed."

She waits for our father to come home. She doesn't go to her room, but sits patiently in the lounge.

Once in our beds, we cannot sleep. The tension in the house is unmistakable. The hairs on my body stand on end. Lili insists on reading, ignoring my complaints about the light. I want to talk, but she says sharply, "Why don't you read a book?" I try reading a Nancy Drew, but Nancy's predictable world suddenly holds no appeal. I lie in bed, listening. I can hear my mother in the lounge, the TV turned on low. Her cigarette smoke wafts into our bedroom as she sits smoking in the dark.

I am on the verge of falling asleep when the screech of tyres jolts me awake. Boomer starts to bark and growl. My father never tries to sneak in when he is late. He is no thief who comes in the middle of the night. Instead he is proud, flagrant.

My mother is ready for him.

I rush out of bed. I have to use the toilet in any case. "Mommy?" I say cautiously, "is everything okay?"

"Go to bed, Danny!" she says sharply. I obey her immediately.

She opens the front door before my father can put his key in the slot. The door opens with a whoosh that blows through the entire house, then is quickly slammed shut again by the wild wind. Lili sits up in bed, rubbing her eyes. We have been waiting for this.

"You bloody no-good bastard," our mother snarls at him, "where were you today?"

It is obvious that our father is stupefied. He is used to avoidance and us walking on eggshells around him. Not this confrontation. In his drunken state, he starts to blubber, but cannot form the right words. Our mother is a virago, a tiger.

"Do you know what's happening in this country, in this very area?

And you leave my children alone!" Her voice is high-pitched, but she is calm. It is an icy rage. The worst kind. She pours out all the resentment she has been feeling for the past few months. She spits out everything she wanted to say, all those times she bit her tongue and kept the peace.

Lili and I look at each other in awe. We cannot believe this. Our father says nothing and for a long, long time there is silence. Absolute silence, like a suspended breath. Then the moment passes and we hear their bedroom door click shut.

♠

"Your father left us," our mother remarks to Lili and me as we walk home from the shops. She could have been discussing the weather, which is unseasonably hot. A berg wind is blowing. We are experiencing the uncanny calm before the heavens burst. It's the kind of day when you rush to get your washing on the line because you know it will dry quickly in the stifling air. As we walk, I take notice of people's gardens, which have burst into life overnight. Bluebells and snowdrops and daffodils stand poised in their flowerbeds, unruffled by the day. I am so busy admiring the pretty flowers that the news doesn't sink in at first.

There had been no warning. No more than usual. After the argument, things settled down and our father didn't leave us alone again. It was as if everything was forgotten. Of course I knew that things were bad and that my family was in trouble, but I thought that everything would work out. That things would go back to the way they were before. That my father was still my father.

I wonder if Lili guessed that this would happen. I quickly glance at her, to check. She is stunned quiet.

Suddenly our mother starts to cry, and we are embarrassed in case anyone sees her. We hurry her home, each of us gripping a hand. She collapses in her chair at the kitchen table. Lili makes her a good cup of tea. Sweet, the way she likes it. Ma always told us that a cup of hot, sweet tea could cure anything. Looking at our mother, we realise that maybe Ma was wrong. Slowly, both of us edge away from her, thinking that she wants to be alone. But she wants to talk.

"You girls are all I have left," she sighs.

Even though I am young, I know it's true. I want to ask her why she is so unhappy about him leaving, but I don't know how. I am unhappy too. My father never said goodbye to me.

I think that it is around this time that Lili and I decide that we need to protect our mother. We lie awake at night and hear her crying in the next room. We stretch out our hands across our beds until they touch. Then we clench our hands together tightly, willing the crying to stop.

Most times, it never stops. I climb into my sister's bed, and we hold each other in our desperation. We believe that if we concentrate really, really hard, the crying will stop. It never does. We fall asleep to the sound of our mother's tears.

Absolution

I am idly paging through a magazine, wishing that I was any place but here, sitting next to my mother, when an intrusive cough breaks my concentration. It is hesitant; a stranger, I can tell without looking up. Not a hospital staffer. The doctors and nurses in their stark white coats enter with a firm tread, with the entitlement that their positions afford them. I look up from the latest fashions, slightly resentful.

"Can I help you?" I ask the man standing at the entrance to the room, a wilting bunch of yellow roses clutched limply in his hand. He is obviously in the wrong place. I scrutinise him: thin, balding, a few years older than Lili. Nondescript.

The man's eyes dart, then lock on my mother's inert form. He ignores me. He seems appalled, transfixed. Maybe he doesn't see me.

"I think you have the wrong room," I tell him, outraged at his audacity.

The man looks at me, really looks, as if trying to place me. I do not know him. I am about to call the nurse when he says, "This is May Matthews's room, isn't it?" Quieter, he adds, "That is, May, I mean . . ." His voice trails off. He looks at me as if beseeching me to tell him that it is not her.

193

"How do you know my mother?" I ask imperiously. I hate surprises.

"My name's Basil," he answers. "I'm a friend of your mother's . . ."

His bashful tone makes me study him more closely. Basil is young, certainly much younger than my mother. Yet there is an older air about him. A sadness, almost. "Mothballed" is the word that comes to mind. He looks like he comes from another era, in his green cardigan and grey pants. His hair is shiny as if gelled back. I can see him and my mother being friends.

"Ah," I say grimly. I have perfected ways to make people uncomfortable if they make me uncomfortable. My properness unnerves them every time.

Basil seems unperturbed by my frostiness. I think that the spectre of my mother as she is now frightens him much more than I ever could. "Didn't your mother mention me?"

"No," I reply. "She liked to keep certain parts of her life private."

Basil looks at me and nods in woeful agreement. "Which one are you?" he asks. Before I answer, he says, "You must be Danika – your mother said you were tall."

"Mmm," I say. "How long have you known my mother?"

"Ah, for over three years now. She is a wonderful woman."

As we talk, he edges further into the room, emboldened by the conversation. He is nearly at the foot of the bed, but still he looks at me. Suddenly, as if wanting to unburden himself, he tells me, "You know, I loved May, your mother, I wanted to marry her, but she wouldn't hear anything of it. A few months ago, she stopped taking my calls and we just lost touch. I found out last week only . . ."

"It's okay," I say, softening. Why let him suffer? I can tell that he is desperate for absolution, and I am feeling magnanimous. "Where did you meet?" I ask.

"At the museum," he says, but he doesn't elaborate.

"Ah yes?" I say.

"Your mother was very proud of you," he offers. "Of both her daughters. She spoke about you all the time."

"Really?" I say. It is not a question. I conceal my discomfort with sarcasm. Listening to this stranger speak about my mother like this brings tears to my eyes. I feel that I am going to lose control, so I excuse myself. "I'm going for a walk," I say. "Maybe you want to be alone with her."

Basil's eyes widen in fear. I know that she is not the woman whom he once knew and, who knows, probably loved. I am willing to give him the benefit of the doubt. "Thank you," he murmurs.

When I come back nearly an hour later, the roses are on the table next to her, but Basil is gone. I wonder if he will visit her again.

Spring Queen

Lili and I have never really known our mother's men. Yet she was never without one. They seldom lasted longer than a month or two. I would tell her that she was scared to be alone, but as usual, she insisted that I was talking nonsense.

Of course, children don't want their divorced parents to date again. But it was more than that. When we were growing up, you would think that our mother was the teenager, not us. She'd slam the phone down on a boyfriend, only for him to call back later and slam the phone in *her* face. They were not prizes, those men.

Before we were old enough to think about dating, my mother told Lili and me the criteria for men. They had to look a certain way and, above all, they had to treat us right.

My mother had no such discernment when it came to herself. It was hard for us to watch her flouting her own rules, and it pained me to see how men treated her. I guess her bar was set quite low. Thankfully she never married again.

When I was at university, I would visit my mother, bring her books to read. The early feminists, books that I'd buy second-hand: Betty Friedan, Nancy Friday, Marilyn French and Gloria Steinem. I wanted her to discover the lessons I believed she should have learnt long before. After all, she had grown up when these very books and the women's movement were at the height of their popularity.

Although she admired the principles, my mother is not a liberated woman. I have often thought that she can only see herself reflected in a man's eyes. I don't know whether she read those books. I never asked.

Disappear

Again, I wonder where my mother's friends are. Too late, I realise I should have asked Basil about this – somebody had to have told him that she was in hospital. He didn't leave a number where I could reach him.

My mother's relationships with her female friends have echoed her relationships with men. She collected the sad, the lonely, the unfortunate, the infirm. Just like her men. People would blow into her life and, for however long they remained part of her world – a week, a few months, a year or two – she would be consumed by them and their problems. She thought that she could save everyone, that no one was beyond redemption.

These friendships followed predictable patterns. Sometimes, to amuse myself, I would identify the various stages. In the courtship phase, she would quickly gain the other person's trust by revealing inappropriate and intimate details of her own life, the gorier the better. Nothing was sacred. Then she would show her compassionate side: "I am just like you." Then, her vulnerability, so that the rescued wanted to become the rescuer.

She would listen to them and feign interest in their insights, but I knew that once she had spoken dismissively of them to me, they were on their way out. Some of them were nice and I'd want to say to them, "Can't you see the signs? Your friendship will not last!" But it was not my place to say anything.

Usually, what signalled the cooling-off was when they dared to offer her advice. Especially when it came to her own relationships with men. She would listen, humouring them, but she would never follow the advice; she would sooner replace the friend than the man. I think, though, that she revelled in their concern. She enjoyed being told that she deserved better.

Bitter tears

Our mother could not understand how both her daughters could be single. We were so young, so pretty. Pointedly, I tried to tell her that I'd rather be single than in a relationship that was bad for me; but she would not get it. Would refuse to understand. I sometimes thought that there was no reaching her. That I would never understand her, nor she me. So instead, I learnt not to say anything.

My mother was never that reticent. She would talk about her failed romances, while averring that she did not believe in love. According to her, men were good for one thing only. I wouldn't want to hear this, but once she was started on men and their shortcomings, there was no stopping her. I would be spared no detail in her quest to have an adult relationship with me. I think that no daughter should know her mother that well – but again, I did not tell her this.

For all her bravado, I watched as men treated my mother with disrespect. And even though I kept quiet, it shamed me to watch my mother abase herself for a man. I would marvel at her unerringly bad taste. She really knows how to pick them, I'd think privately. I had learnt not to voice my opinions. I marvelled at the amount of power she ceded to them. Willingly. Although for some strange reason, I think Basil might have been different.

I would placate her when she worried about her looks, her age, her desirability. But I did these things quietly. I learnt that when I tried to champion her cause, tell her that she deserved better treatment, I would become the enemy. Instead of being flattered she became defensive, denying any mistreatment. If anyone's heart was being broken, it was not hers. She was the heartbreaker! In her mind, she was still the prettiest girl in class. How could Lili and I ever compete with that?

No one likes a mirror held up to their lives, I guess. So I learnt to be subtle. When I could not be subtle, I would find refuge in being polite, distant. Let her live her own life, I thought. But I never stopped worrying.

On the rare occasions that I saw her cry bitter tears, I felt embarrassed by her defeat. She was defeated by the usual: age, and a life that showed on her body and in her face.

One day, my mother let me down for a man once too many. I was so angry, I swore that this would be the last time. She didn't bother to come up with a plausible or even flamboyant excuse.

"One day you will look for me and I won't be there!" I yelled. "One day, you will be all alone and need me. The men who you are always throwing your children away for won't want you!" I spat, wounding her by voicing her biggest fear. Some small, mean part of me wanted to draw blood. And tears.

"I will never need you," my mother retorted, turning her back and walking away, effectively ending the conversation.

Years later, as I wipe my mother's brow with a face cloth dipped in lavender water, my words come back to me.

"You needed me after all," I whisper.

It is a hollow victory.

Spring 1985

The night after my father leaves, I am awoken by the clicking sound the front door makes when it is unlatched. "Daddy's home!" I think to myself. I am so excited that I race out of bed, though I can barely keep my eyes open. Without bothering to put my slippers on, I run outside.

Instead of my father, I find my mother, dressed in a short nightie. What will the neighbours think if they see her? It is cold and the ground is wet. It has been raining, the soft, gentle rain of spring.

"What are you doing, Mommy?" I ask, confused.

"Killing snails," she replies as she sprinkles salt on the ground.

I watch the snails recoil as soon as the salt hits their exposed parts. With some satisfaction, I note the seething, sizzling sounds they make.

On Sunday evening, our mother tells us that we'll have to stay at Ma's house because it is not safe for us to stay alone at home. Lili and I realise this, so we don't argue. We know that bad things are happening. It is no longer an abstract.

She tells us to pack a lot of clothes because she doesn't know how long we will have to stay. Who knows anything these days? Ma is coming to fetch us because our father has taken the car. Our mother is especially cross about this, since she paid for the car to be fixed the last time.

Ma comes just as it's starting to get dark. Our bags have been packed and waiting for hours. We hear her car pull up – the creaking old Valiant makes a lot of noise. She jauntily hoots to announce her arrival, in case we didn't hear. Slowly she makes her way up the path.

"Your Cape may's growing nicely," she tells our mother, who is waiting at the front door. Our mother told us that Ma bought her this tree when we first moved into our house. She jokes that she was named after the tree, as it has always been Ma's favourite. My mother prefers fruit trees, but the Cape may is watered and pruned on time.

"Thanks, Mommy," my mother says. "Come inside; we'll have some tea and cake."

My mother makes a cake every Sunday afternoon, no matter what. Today she made Ma's favourite, coconut and jam tarts. I helped her roll out the pastry. You would never say that anything was wrong. My mother is so calm, I have to rack my memory to make sure my father really left us yesterday. I wonder what she told Ma.

Lili and I follow them to the kitchen, where the teapot has been in readiness all afternoon. As soon as our mother sees us, she says, "Lili, will you and Danika put your bags in Ma's car? I want to talk to Ma in private."

I can tell that Lili is cross about being excluded, but she's trying to be helpful. "Come, Danny, let's see that we have everything."

Ma and our mother do not speak for long. Our mother makes us pack the leftover tarts to take with us. She hugs us tightly before we go. "I'll see you girls on Friday evening," she says. "I'll come straight after work."

We are in the car, waving, when Lili asks quietly, "Ma, do you think my mommy will be okay?"

"Of course she will! Don't be silly," Ma says.

Our mother remains outside in the road until the car turns the corner and we can no longer see her.

Ma's house is old and rickety, unlike our house, which is modern. Our house has wall-to-wall carpeting; Ma's house has no carpets. Only wooden floors that we are forced to polish on our hands and knees with lavender polish and dirty, gritty cloths that do little more than smear the dirt around. Polishing is no use if you don't sweep properly. I hate housework and this is backbreaking! I grumble all the time, but Ma takes no notice.

"In my day, children were spoken to and not heard," she silences me. "I had to spread mis on my grandmother's kitchen floor and polish it until it shone. Do you know what mis is?"

I do not believe her when she tells me that mis is cow dung, and that people actually put it on their floors. "It was so warm," she says, "and didn't smell at all!"

I think that it is just a story to scare me into doing my work. If she liked it so much, then why doesn't she have a mis floor in her house?

The food, too, is different. During the week, Ma buys brown bread only. The texture of "government loaf" is as gritty as the polish rags. She cuts the bread into thick doorstop slices. On them, we spread whatever jam she has recently made. Mulberry or gooseberry jam made from fruit from the garden, otherwise just plain apricot jam. Or we have konfyt on our bread.

I hate having to prick the hard melon to make this delicacy, the tines of the fork often catch the sides of my hands. I cannot help but think that the finished product isn't worth all the hard work. The konfyt is sickly sweet. Ma tells us how much Auntie Astrid and our cousins in Canada love it. It is mainly for them that she makes it. She bottles it in plastic jars, which are wrapped and put in the suitcase of anyone she knows (or who knows someone she knows) who is going to Canada.

"Why don't you write down the recipe?" she suggests. "You like writing so much. One day when I'm gone, you'll be able to make it yourself."

I don't think it's likely that I'll ever want to make konfyt, but I humour her. Lili, who is still pricking the melon, glares at me. She's older

and by rights she should be the one taking down the recipe; but perhaps my complaints and exaggerated pain from the inadvertent fork
stabbings are trying Ma's patience. I smile triumphantly at Lili as Ma
painstakingly instructs me in the fine art of konfyt-making.

"You have to get a medium-sized konfyt melon. Like this one," she
says. "Then you cut it into squares and take the skin off. You can cut up
the inside for melon and ginger jam. It's the hard rind that you use for
the konfyt."

I know all of this. I have watched her make konfyt many times before.

"Then you have to prick the squares of rind all over." She nods at
Lili, who glares at me behind Ma's back. "Once the melon is pricked,
add a heaped teaspoon of slaked lime to a large basin of water. I buy
the lime from the chemist. Then swirl it around in the bowl to mix."

"Then what?" I ask Ma.

"Then you put the pricked pieces in the bowl, of course." Ma looks
at me as if I haven't been paying attention. "Leave it to stand overnight,
but remember to turn it when you get up to use the toilet during the
night."

"What if you don't get up?" Lili asks smartly.

Ma pretends that she doesn't hear her. "Then, the next day, rinse the
lime off and put the squares in a big pot with water and slivers of green
ginger and bring it to the boil. After fifteen minutes, turn it around.

Take the pieces out and divide them into two bowls. Put what was on top at the bottom and what was at the bottom on top."

"Why, Ma?" I ask. This seems like too much hard work.

"So that it can be evenly browned," Ma explains. "Then, after about half an hour, put in a kilogram or so of sugar and bring to the boil. Be careful not to let the sugar burn."

"And then, Ma?"

"Turn it around again, like before. Stir it quite often so that it's even. It is ready when it's golden and bright. Then you can take it out of the pot and lay it on a flat dish to cool and dry. But don't let the pieces touch," she warns, "or they'll stick together."

"Is that all?" I ask, already bored.

"Yes," Ma says with a sigh. "It worries me that you girls aren't interested in the old ways."

I don't particularly like konfyt, but the next day, when the rich smell of ginger wafts through the house, fragrancing the air, I can't wait for it to be done. My mouth waters. I cannot wait to bite into the hard, glassy shell of the block of konfyt and taste the sticky, sweet insides.

Ma is a frugal woman. Every night, she scours the newspapers for coupons that Lili and I will have to redeem the next day. No matter how unsafe she tells us it is to venture out onto the stoep, it is always fine for us to go to the shops for her. We walk from shop to shop to buy the various specials advertised in the newspaper. "And check the price per kilo," she warns. "Make sure it's the one advertised!"

Always, she tells us how much we have to be grateful for. "I grew up during the war, you know. If you girls had lived through that, you would never waste."

"Ma, is there going to be a war?" I ask. She ignores me, since she is on her favourite subject: how much she has suffered. We have heard the stories so many times, we know them by heart.

"There were so many of us; my mother never had enough to feed us. We used to get two slices of bread that my mother had to make the night before, and all we had to spread on it was a smearing of fat."

"Gross!" I exclaim, well aware of the horrors of the fat bakkie. In this, Ma keeps the fat that she skims off whatever food she's making. It's not unusual to have curry-flavoured roast potatoes, or fish that tastes like meat.

"What to you mean, gross?" she says. "Do you know how much we loved it?" She continues before I can say anything more. "It was a real treat when my mother allowed us to sprinkle sugar on top of the fat, but that was only on a Sunday. There was nothing better. You girls are so spoilt," she concludes. "You don't know how lucky you have it!"

I for one am tired of people telling me that I am lucky. I don't feel lucky at all.

♠

At night we all pile into Ma's bed. I'm squashed in the middle between Lili and Ma, who always insists that we are thoroughly clean before we are allowed into her bed. "Have you washed your feet? Did you brush your teeth?"

The bed is not like our mother's snug cocoon. Our mother sleeps in the middle when Lili and I argue about who gets to sleep on the end. We both want to be the one to sleep next to our mother.

I hate sleeping next to Ma – she snores loudly in her sleep and it scares me. I lie gasping for air because the blankets are pushed up so high. I try pushing them away, but she and Lili hike them up in their sleep. I cannot breathe and I cannot sleep. I miss my home and my bed. I wonder if my father has come back home yet.

Auntie Astrid calls from Canada almost every day now. She is worried about all of us because Cape Town and the riots were on their TV again. When she calls, we are shooed out of the room so that Ma can talk in peace. (International telephone calls are very expensive, we know.) Ma talks so loudly, repeating everything that Auntie Astrid says, that we hear the news anyway: "Really, Astrid, the police were beating up demonstrators in Athlone, you say? What? You recognised Athlone?"

Our mother calls every night too, since she can visit us only on weekends. She finishes work too late, she says. And she has to take a different train line to Ma's house. Every time we speak, I ask her if my father has returned. Every time it's the same answer, until I learn to stop asking. The question makes our mother sad, and Lili and Ma exchange looks when I ask it. Instead, I ask her about Boomer.

♠

"Waste not, want not," Ma tells me and Lili.

We have heard this many times before. She throws nothing away. We look at each other when she gives us soft bananas; both of us like eating mashed banana on our bread, but these are brown and have a pungent, overripe smell.

"But it's brown, Ma," Lili says, stating the obvious.

I keep quiet, pretending to be interested in something on the floor.

"So?" Ma asks, daring Lili to say more. "Just cut off the brown bits."

I glance at Lili out of the corner of my eye, trying to convey to her the inherent danger in this conversation. That she should stop complaining. Neither of us want to hear any more of Ma's stories about the war.

"Shall I make the tea, Ma?" I offer. I've been allowed to make tea by myself since the beginning of this year.

Ma nods in surprise. It is usually Lili's job to make the tea, but Lili is being difficult.

I search among the various pieces of crockery for a matching set. Ma is not like the other grandmothers, with their fancy tea sets and every-thing just so.

There is at least one matching cup and saucer, in a blue willow pattern. This is reserved for Ma. It holds just the right amount of tea, she says. I open the flask, careful not to burn myself, then rinse the cups with the boiled water. To save electricity, Ma boils the kettle in the morning and puts the water in the flask, which sits on the kitchen table. Usually, the water is more than enough for the whole day; we pour any leftover water into the washing-up basin.

Then I put the teabag into Ma's cup and add the one teaspoon of sugar that she allows herself as a treat. Lili and I have to share a teabag. Should we complain and demand our own teabags, Ma will once more remind us how lucky we are. She says that when she was younger, there was no such thing as teabags. Her mother made tea in a pot with loose tea-leaves. Until the day she turned fifteen, she was allowed to have half a cup of tea only. She tells me and Lili the story of how proud she was that first day, drinking her full cup of tea with her birthday cake.

I add the milk and give the cup a stir, but I leave the teabag in – the way Ma likes it. As I pass the tea over to Ma, I am careful not to spill.

"Thank you, my girl," is the only reward for my efforts, but I glow. It is usually Lili whom Ma calls "my girl".

♠

It is Friday night. We anxiously await our mother's visit. She takes a train from Town, as she no longer works in the factory. The owner had to close it down, but he managed to get her and some of the other workers jobs at his son's firm in Town. It is a clothing company too, but not a factory; it's a chain of clothing stores. Our mother's job is as supervisor of the collections department. More important than her old job, she tells us, and a bit more money. Soon, she will be able to buy herself a car.

Lili and I ask Ma if we can wait on the station for our mother. "I'll go with you," she says. "It's not safe for you girls to go by yourselves."

We walk to Wittebome station, which is five minutes away, excited to see her. Ma smiles indulgently at the two of us. Our mother is not on the first train. Nor the second. We wait and wait. Eventually Ma says that we should go back home and wait for her there.

When we get back to Ma's house, our mother is standing on the stoep. "I decided to buy fish and chips at Castletown Fisheries, so I got off at Wynberg station," she explains, the hot parcel still in her hands. I run over to hug my mother; she smells of warm vinegar.

"Let's go inside and eat, before the food gets cold," Ma says, fiddling in the pocket of her cardigan for her key. "May, you should have told me that you were going to get supper," she scolds my mother. "I made pumpkin bredie."

"Ag, you can have it tomorrow," my mother says brightly.

I am glad for the fish and chips. I don't like Ma's bredies because the meat she puts in is not nice. If it is not too bony, it's too fatty.

"Go and wash your hands, girls," Ma tells me and Lili.

After supper, Ma and our mother sit smoking their cigarettes while Lili and I wash the dishes.

"The schools are going to be opened again," our mother announces through a wisp of smoke.

"What's that you said?" Ma asks with a splutter.

I'm so shocked, I drop the cup I am busy drying. It cracks and breaks on the hard floor. No one takes any notice of this, or of me as I pick up the pieces of the shattered cup.

"So when do the children go back to school?" Ma asks the question that all of us want to know. "On Monday, then?"

"No, Mommy, it's still supposed to be school holidays now. The official school term starts on the first of October."

"Since when are they interested in doing things official?" Ma asks. "What made it official for them to close the schools in the first place? They are not even my official government!" Ma says bitterly.

"Yes, Mommy, I know," our mother consoles her.

"Are you going to sleep here?" Lili asks our mother, breaking the tension.

"No, my girl," she answers, looking at the two of us as if noticing us for the first time. "I have to go to a meeting tonight. A friend of mine is going to fetch me here."

Ma raises her eyebrows and flashes her a dirty look. Our mother gives her a pleading look. "Please, Mom," she says. "It's important."

♠

As Ma says, time flies. Soon it is time for us to go back home and back to school. I wish that the holiday would never end, although I miss my mother and home. Lili can't wait to go back to school and see all her friends. I think it is the boys she wants to see.

The funny thing is, we won't go back to school on the first like we're supposed to. Our mother and Ma decide that we should go back on the second, just to show them that they cannot make decisions about people's lives. Everyone is doing it, Ma says.

The day before we are to go back home, our mother calls and tells Ma about the helicopter that circled above the houses early that morning, waking all the people who were still sleeping. Ma relates the news as we eat our breakfast: "A policeman in the helicopter used a loudhailer to tell the people to behave themselves when the schools open tomorrow. Can you believe the nerve of them?"

Lili and I carry on eating and say nothing. Ma doesn't need a reply. Later on, we know that she will go outside and tell all her neighbours. Those of them who agree with her and those who don't.

♠

It is the afternoon and Ma is lying down to rest before she has to make our supper. Lili and I are playing outside so that we don't make a noise and disturb her. We take turns climbing the trees. I am a student and Lili is a policeman who's trying to arrest me. Wynberg is strangely silent.

We notice the smoke before we hear the noise. We can see the growing clouds from the back yard. The smoke is thick and black. It chokes us and gets in our hair and our clothes. Still, we don't know for certain what's happening.

"Go get our handkerchiefs," Lili orders me. We are supposed to always keep a handkerchief on us, in case of the smoke, but we always forget.

"What is it?" I ask Lili. "Do you think it's tear gas?"

"Don't be silly!"

Once we have placed the wetted handkerchiefs over our mouths and noses, we try to see what's happening by climbing the tall trees in the garden – but with little success.

I run inside, waking Ma. "Ma, come see the smoke!"

Ma complains sleepily, but she comes outside. "What is it?" she says, grumbling but alert. "Lili?"

Then we hear the singing. First from far away, then louder. "We shall overcome." The three of us look at one another, frozen. Eventually, Lili runs to the low wall.

"There's hundreds, thousands of them!" she cries excitedly.

"Come away from there!" Ma screams at Lili, who is clearly torn between Ma's instructions and the uneasy thrill of the procession at the bottom of the road.

"Get inside!" Ma pushes us into the house and starts locking the doors and windows.

Ma lights a cigarette and nervously puffs on it. "Put the kettle on, my girl," she tersely tells Lili. "I think we can all do with a cup of tea."

Although we are scared, Lili and I devise strategies by which one of us will escape Ma's vigilant watch in order to see what is going on. But Ma calls out as soon as she hears one of us touch the latch of the front door. Her hearing is uncanny and her eyes are everywhere. As soon as we start whispering, she is there, with her wet kitchen cloth in her hand. She doesn't have to say anything; she just glares meaningfully at us and then at the wet cloth. We know what this means. Although we have not felt the sting of the wet cloth, we know all about it from the stories Ma tells us about her own grandmother.

Ma cannot contain herself. After her cigarette, she goes to phone from her bedroom. I stealthily open the front door and venture out. It is deathly silent outside, like a ghost town, not the busy suburb we know. The only noise is an unfamiliar rumbling in the distance. Then the screams.

I scoot into the spreading loquat tree next to the stoep. I can climb high in this tree; I'll be able to see what's going on, maybe tell Lili something she doesn't know. As I climb, I can feel someone watching me, and I freeze. It's a young man, walking past the house, wearing what I think is an army uniform. He smiles shyly when our eyes meet and puts his finger to his mouth. Ssh! I smile back; he has such gentle blue eyes, he looks like a prince in one of my storybooks.

As soon as he is gone, I rush into the house to tell Lili. But she is not impressed. She knows who our enemies are. She tells on me: "Ma, Danny spoke to a soldier."

Ma turns to look at me, stoops, her eyes bulging. "Don't you ever speak to those pigs again!" she warns. "If only you knew what they do to children!"

I wonder how the handsome young man could be a pig. He was so nice to me. And what are the soldiers doing to children? But I don't say anything. Instead, I walk away and find a place where I can cry.

Soon we will be back home.

This must be the place I waited years to leave

I touch the surfaces of my childhood home, skimming my hands over walls, windowsills, as the ghosts of my memory dance before me. Every scratch on the kitchen table, every creaking chair: I know it. As my fingers trail dust, I think of the silent spectre that has haunted me throughout my life. Even now. It is not how messed up my mother was or whether Lili liked me. It is my father.

For so long I have blotted him out. Whoever said we can never forget? Forgetting is easy. It is remembering that is hard. I hate this age of therapy. Of working out our problems. TV talk shows and self-help books. Blaming our parents. Still, when I consider the barren landscape of my life, I wonder. If only my father . . . If only.

Everything in this house overwhelms me, so I walk outside to check on the garden, which is my pretext for coming here after all. The fresh air hits me after the stuffiness inside. The sun dapples through the overgrown ivy and makes gentle patterns on the paving. The lawn and the trees disappeared years ago. Only a small patch of neglected grass remains. Everything is overgrown, gone to seed.

I walk from container to container, my mother's preferred form of gardening. Here and there I can see an iris or a freesia stalk pushing its way through the dry soil. It has been years since I gardened. Not even potted herbs survive the heat of my flat. Still, I can differentiate the plants by looking at their stalks. It makes sense: my mother never pulled up her bulbs once they had flowered. She would allow the foliage to die down, leaving them in the ground for the next year. Nature has taken over now.

I feel like an intruder in my mother's garden. This is her world. I don't belong here any more. Her life is so exposed, I feel uncomfortable; I don't want to discover anything more. Let our parents remain a mystery, I think – although once I needed to understand.

My discomfort is so great that I don't bother to make myself the cup of tea I was planning, though the water has boiled. Not like there is milk anyway. Instead, I water the pot plants, willing life into those that look hopeless. Who knows?

Relative stranger

Our father's departure from our lives was absolute. There was no lingering. One day he was there, the next he wasn't. He made no attempt to see Lili and me after he left. Or at least, I don't think he did.

Sometimes the phone would ring late at night, creating a static buzz in the air. If I was in bed (and I often was), I would shrug off the tangled sheets and blankets and fly to be the one to answer the phone. Across the room, Lili, reading by the weak glow of her bedside lamp, would glower at me. Whenever I reached the phone first, the person on the other end would click off as soon as I answered. But usually my mother would answer, and have a long conversation in hushed tones.

"Is it Daddy?" I'd ask, pulling on her legs and struggling to pull the receiver away from her clenched hands. "I want to speak to Daddy."

"Sssh, go sleep!" my mother would hiss in the same low, urgent voice she used for conducting these late-night conversations. "This is not your father."

I wondered why our father never visited or phoned us. Not even on our birthdays or Christmas. His parents and siblings never phoned either. Can a parent so completely forget his children? I wondered what we had done to make him stop loving us. I wished I didn't miss him.

Did my mother speak to my father, I wonder? Try to get him to see us or call us? When I was younger, she would forge his name on my birthday cards, until one day I realised that it was her handwriting.

Five years later, I did see him. It was a Saturday morning – at the supermarket, of all places. I had gone alone with our mother, as Lili considered herself too old to go shopping with us. My mother let me push the trolley, and flattered me by making a big deal about consulting me on the household purchases. I was about to turn into the fruit and vegetable section when I saw him.

Pushing a heavily laden trolley, a chubby toddler squashed into the child seat. A pale, chubby toddler. I saw him smile at the child indulgently as he stopped beside a lush display of fruit. Then a lady with a bright red perm came over to him, her outstretched hands each clutching a sweet melon for his deliberation. He put one, then the other to his nose to smell which was the riper.

The aching familiarity of this gesture brought something very close to the surface. I could not breathe. Swiftly, I turned the trolley around before my mother could see.

"We forgot something in the other aisle," I lied.

Father figure

A small part of me is relieved that my father is gone. A few years ago – I was in my first year of university at the time – Ma Matthews called my mother to let us know that he had died. So this is not new, the death of a parent. But that wasn't personal. Not like this. Can adults be orphans?

Surprisingly, I found myself able to feel sympathy for my father. As I would for anyone who died the way he did.

As far as we know, his body was found on a field behind Retreat station, near his parents' house. Presumably murdered, perhaps stabbed, although the police could not be sure. His body had been lying there for a long time. No one reported him missing until a good few days had passed. He was good at getting lost, going missing. We found out that he'd been living back home with his parents. No one mentioned any other family. Or what he had been doing in the intervening years. Some things are better left unsaid.

My mother said she accepted the news of his death calmly and thanked Ma Matthews for letting her know. She said that there was a prickly silence during the telephone call. What was she expecting – hysteria, tears? What was there for any of us to mourn? The relationship that never was? What could have been?

We later discovered that he was not working and had been living on handouts for many years before it happened. He was forty-four at the time of his death. From the things that were said and that were not said, we surmised that the booze had taken over his life. One of his sisters told my mother accusingly that at times he had slept in a broken-down car and sometimes at a night shelter.

He had let his hair grow long, and his nails were black . . . that is only my imagination. Perhaps his skin was red and blotched, the florid complexion of street people whom I see, but do not see. I never knew for sure. The coffin was going to be closed and there would be a small ceremony for family only. He would have wanted us there, Ma Matthews said.

I had nightmares of him harassing me when I was out with friends in my smart little ensembles with everything matched just so, and my understated but expensive jewellery. Living the good life.

Would I be ashamed of him, pretend that I didn't know him? Or would I stop to say hello? I know. I would walk away, staring straight ahead. Our eyes would never meet.

Why should I care?

My mother insisted on attending the funeral. I went along for moral support. It was hard to be polite to this so-called family of mine. Not that they made any attempt to be nice to me. Lili decided that she was not going to be a hypocrite (her words) and stayed away.

"He really missed you girls," Ma Matthews told me, clasping my hands and looking heartsore and bereft.

He had a good way of showing it, I thought, but didn't say anything. I did, however, decline to attend the tea afterwards. Let them think what they want, I reasoned.

The only good that came out of it all was that one of my lecturers gave me an extension for an essay I was struggling with, due to my "bereavement".

Spring 1985

It is strange to be back at school after the long break. The first day, our mother walks us to school. We have to go through the main gate. All the other gates are closed. There is a man in front at the main gate who asks our names and classes. Our mother stares at him insolently and clicks her tongue in annoyance, but she says nothing.

Our principal is standing in front of his office, watching the gate. He comes over to us, sensing trouble. "Is everything okay, Mrs Matthews?" he asks with a smile.

"I didn't know the school was worried about security?" she asks.

Mr Charles shrugs and takes hold of her arm, taking her away from the man at the gate. "We weren't consulted," he offers. "The government decided that we needed a security guard."

He winks at us knowingly. All men like our mother.

"Be good," she says as we leave to go to our classrooms. "Ma is going to fetch you this afternoon, so wait for her here in front."

We nod our heads vigorously. We cannot wait to get back to our classrooms and our friends. There is so much catching up to do.

♠

The next day, our mother tells us that we cannot stay at home by ourselves and that Ma cannot fetch us every day. She will have to hire a domestic helper to look after us during the day while she is at work.

Flora is an older lady of at least forty. She is the nicest person you can get. She calls Lili and me "Madam". It is not like when Ma Matthews called us "madams". We like it. We find it very funny, because she is a grown-up and she calls us Madam. Until our mother overhears this and swiftly puts a stop to it. She says that we must respect Flora as she is a grown woman with children of her own.

Lili tells our mother that we are too old to need a babysitter. Our mother raises her eyebrows at this. I don't say too much, because it is nice to have Flora around. It is nice to have someone else to clean the dishes and vacuum the carpets. And all the other things that Lili and I don't like to do.

Flora has two sons in high school. She confides in Lili and me how worried she is about them. "They are good boys," she says, "but ooh, the things that are happening in the location where I live."

We press her for more details, but I think she has been warned by my mother not to tell us too much.

♠

Now that our father is gone, Lili and I have to be very careful around our mother. Anything we say or do can make her snap at us. Or cry. I can handle her snapping much better than I can her crying. We have to be really careful that we do not mention our father. She says that we are forbidden even to say his name in the house.

The only person who is allowed to mention him is her, it seems. "Stop doing that," she will tell Lili or me. "You're just like your father."

This is the worst fate that can befall either of us. There is so much power in the curse that when Lili torments me, I shout, "Mommy, Lili's being just like my father!" Although Lili glares at me, I know that before long she will accuse me of the same. The ultimate insult.

I scrutinise my face in the mirror, looking for any traces of my father. I agonise over my button nose, upset that it is not the sharp "Roman" nose of my mother. Of which my father was so proud.

Sometimes Lili and I make up a game that we are from different fathers. We enjoy the game so much that we start telling our friends about it. It is easy to believe, because while Lili is quite fair, I am dark by comparison. We enjoy this game so much until someone's mother, eager for the gossip, asks our mother whether it is true. Our mother is very angry when she confronts the two of us. "Just what do you want people to think of me?" she demands. We don't know why she is so upset.

♠

"I don't care what the neighbours think," my mother says with defiance; yet where we live, what the neighbours think is paramount. Their eyes and ears are everywhere. Do something differently, like let your lawn grow an inch longer than you used to, and you'll soon hear about it. "Shame, is there something wrong with your lawnmower?" someone will ask.

Houses are painted regularly in respectable colours like white, cream or, if you really want to stand out, yellow. Usually only the Moslem houses are dressed in flamboyant hues like turquoise, green or maroon. Every night, you close the curtains at a decent hour for privacy and you don't make a noise after dark. In fact, you try not to make any noise at all.

On Saturdays, the wives and children go shopping while the men tinker with their cars or their lawns. Women who can't drive either take a bus or the train to the shopping centre, or their husbands take them shopping on Friday evenings after work. My mother prefers to go early on a Saturday morning, before we are up. Then the food is fresher and there are no crowds.

There is a sameness and predictability that binds us together. But what is happening in the "townships", which I think refers to all the places that are not as nice as where we live, is rapidly spreading dissent through our community.

There is talk of a consumer boycott, but nobody really takes it seriously. My mother tries, but the momentum is not that strong and soon she is back to buying from the usual shops. Auntie Ruthie offers my mother her opinion of the "skollies" in the townships, who are making so much trouble, but my mother has stopped trying to reason with her.

All she is interested in are her paintings. The lounge is the best room for painting in. Something about the light. Sometimes, when there is no light and Lili and I want to watch TV, we try to assert ourselves, but we are no match for the muse. We plead with her to allow us to stay and watch TV. Try to convince her that the noise will not disturb her. We will turn the sound down . . . but we know that all our begging is in vain.

My mother paints her violence on the canvas. Thick, angry strokes of red and black and yellow. Her music is on – loud – echoing through the house. Her favourite song is "Wooden Ships" by Crosby, Stills, Nash & Young. She plays it over and over again. How Lili and I hate that song! We will not find rest here tonight.

Although we are upset that we can't watch TV, we are relieved when our mother paints. She is happiest when she is painting. She hums along with the music, running a paint-splattered hand through her hair. I like to watch her. She is so preoccupied that she doesn't notice me standing in the doorway. She wears a light Indian print dress with swirling purple and red patterns to paint in. I love the way the silver and gold threads in the fabric shimmer in the light.

Usually, we are not allowed to disturb her. She tells me that I ask too many questions and she cannot concentrate. I am cross when she calls

Lili to look at her paintings. Lili preens and struts and feels terribly important. She likes to offer her opinion, like it counts.

"You think you're so smart," I tell her, hurt.

"You're just jealous because she never asked you!" Lili says unkindly and prances out of the room.

♠

Our mother decides that she needs to buy a car. She has to take a bus to Claremont and then a train to Town to get to work now. The bus service is unreliable, she says, and the buses are so full by the time they reach her stop. "What can you expect with what's happening around here? Buses are being targeted in the townships . . ."

Noticing our eager, hungry-for-information faces, she reconsiders.

She scours the classified section of the paper for days until she finds a car that she can afford. She brings only the classified section with her from work. The rest of the paper is discarded before she gets home. In less than two weeks, we are the proud owners of a bright yellow Beetle. The previous owner was leaving the country and "almost gave the car away", our mother says.

"Please take us for a ride," Lili and I beg.

We climb into the car and our mother drives to Ma to show her. "It is my first own car," she says as she drives, her sunglasses perched flirtatiously on her head. "The first car that is mine alone."

"Will you teach me to drive, Mommy?" Lili asks, always pushing, always trying her luck.

Our mother smiles at her fondly. "Of course, my girl, but you must wait until you are sixteen."

Lili turns around to make sure that I heard. She flashes me a look of pure triumph. I smile back at her, pretending not to care. But inside, I fume. It is so unfair! Lili always gets to do everything first. This does not dampen my happiness at the new car, though.

♠

I cannot sleep. I am convinced that there is someone walking on the roof. Walking, running, trying to break in. The noise keeps me awake. Lili is fast asleep. How can she not hear it?

"Psst, Lili," I whisper. I am quiet in case the robbers hear that I am awake. "Did you hear that?"

Unbelievably, Lili does not wake up. The noise does not stop. It sounds like whoever is out there is in the ceiling and not on the roof. Any minute, I expect someone to come crashing through. Crashing down on top of me. Panicked, I shake Lili awake.

She is not impressed. "What do you think you're doing, you little shit?" she demands, so angry that she uses the s-word.

The fear of being attacked makes me brave. "There's somebody on the roof," I whisper, "I think they're trying to get in."

Lili listens, but whoever is there must have heard us and is silent. Lili is now fully awake. The silence stretches out.

Yet I know that I had heard a noise.

"Don't you ever, ever wake me for something so stupid again, you little brat," Lili threatens me. She turns her back to me, angry. Soon she is asleep again. I lie awake, listening.

The next night, the noise returns. It is so loud and so close, I am convinced that Lili must be able to hear it. She does not wake up. I decide to take my chances and wake my mother. This is very risky because she works very hard and needs her sleep.

"Mommy, Mommy," I murmur, "there's someone there, I think they're in the roof!"

My mother is instantly awake. She listens, and this time the noise does not go away. "Go to bed, my girl," she tells me. "It's just a cat walking on the roof. They're probably on heat."

I go to bed, comforted by the thought that it is only a cat up there. Yet the noise still keeps me awake. Now, instead of a person falling through the ceiling into my bedroom, I imagine a cat.

The next morning, Lili smirks at me over her bowl of cereal. She is all fresh and scrubbed, ready for school. I overslept. Our mother has left for work already.

"I hear you woke Mommy up last night," she says with a disgusted look on her face. "You're such a baby!"

I take no notice of her. I stare out of the kitchen window as I rinse my bowl.

"I hear she told you that there were cats in the ceiling – but they are too big to get in. It's probably rats. Haven't you heard of roof rats? That's why they call them roof rats."

I am so stunned by her suggestion that I spin around, forgetting that I'm supposed to be ignoring her. Now that she mentions it, I am sure that I have heard the words "roof" and "rat" together.

Sensing my panic, Lili adds, "I hear them too, scurrying and squeaking. They probably have babies. Be careful, just now they find a way out of the roof."

Catching sight of my terror, Lili sashays out of the room. Victorious.

I wish my father was here.

♠

Our mother comes home from work, her eyes red and swollen. We can tell that she has been crying. When we ask her what's wrong, she doesn't want to talk about it. She stares blankly at us, smoking one cigarette after the other.

Later, she pours herself a glass of wine. I think that she is going to paint, and I follow her to the lounge. Instead, she walks back to the kitchen and starts to prepare supper. That night we have our favourite: steak, chips and salad. As Lili and I clean the kitchen, we hear her on the phone, talking softly. So softly that we cannot hear what she is saying.

We are both nearly asleep when she comes into our room. She stands in the doorway and looks at us attentively, as if she is trying to burn our faces in her memory. She says nothing, just stands and watches us.

The next morning, we wake up and there is a new painting on the easel. It is a picture of children, but not of us. The children are not happy and smiling. Rather, they look as if they have been slaughtered. Lying on the ground in pools of blood, wearing school uniforms. There is a large truck in the background. I cannot understand why our mother would want to paint such an ugly picture. Why doesn't she paint us?

That morning is even more unusual. She makes us pancakes for breakfast, and for once is not worried about the time.

♠

Another day, our mother is angry when she gets home from work. Lili asks her what is wrong. Uncharacteristically, she tells us about her day.

"Our office is very cold," our mother explains, "and Auntie Edwina and I decided to walk to the Gardens to eat our lunch. When we got outside, there was a group of women protesting about the police in the townships."

She takes a sip of tea, her eyes far away, as if she were back there. Lili and I flutter over her. We are eager to hear what she has to say.

"Auntie Edwina and I decided to stay and see what would happen. Then the police came in Casspirs and told us to go back to work. But we stayed. They cannot tell us what to do."

"And then, Mommy?" Lili asks.

Our mother shudders and sighs. "Then the police started whipping the people. And with their new water cannons, spraying purple dye at the crowds."

Lili and I gasp in admiration and shock to think that our mother had been so close to the action.

"We went back to the office, before things got out of hand. It was so confusing, girls, that I lost my sandwiches. We didn't have time to eat. People were pushing and shoving one another out of the way as they tried to escape the whip of the water."

"Sjoe, Mommy," I say nervously.

Our mother carries on. "One of the women I work with, Kathy, told me that it's our fault if we allow our children to riot and carry on like skollies. Can you believe it? She doesn't know what she is talking about!"

Our mother slams her fist down onto the kitchen table, further shattering the Formica. "What does she know!" she says again, bitterly. Then, burying her head in her hands, she starts to cry.

"It's okay, Mommy," I say, patting her on her leg.

It's all I can say, over and over again.

Supernatural

I am sleeping, but in that peculiar state of alertness we assume in times like these, when it jumps on my bed. I am aware of it bounding across the room before launching itself up, yet it is the weight on my feet that wakes me.

Instinctively, I snap on my bedside lamp. In the lit-up room, the two of us stare at each other, frozen. Then I scream at the intrusion. The outrage.

I have always hated cats. Thought they were evil. Its molten yellow eyes glow in the pool of light on my bed. Unflinching. Unwavering. Daring me to blink first. The scream is involuntary and insensitive to my neighbours through the thin, hollow walls of my flat.

The cat – black, angry, alive – glares at me, jumps off the bed, loping languidly across the carpeted floor and out of the open door.

I am still sitting up in bed when it hits me: how did it get in? The awareness prickles the hairs on the back of my neck. I live high up, and am so paranoid about my safety that I do not leave a single window even slightly open at night.

I jump out of bed, determined to find the intruder; search under tables and chairs, behind the fridge. Everywhere. There is no cat. Everything is locked and as it should be. How did it get out? How did it get in?

I open my front door. My next-door neighbour, with whom I am on greeting terms, is outside his with a poised baseball bat. Before he can say anything, I ask, "Have you seen the cat?"

"What cat?" he asks, confused. "You know there are no pets allowed."

But there was a cat. If I had not switched on the light and seen it, rather than merely feeling or sensing it, I would not be as certain. For confirmation, I finger the old cat-scratch scar that I've had since I was a child. I know that the cat was real.

Would you like to talk about it?

I wake up tired the next day. Not sure how or when I got back to sleep. I kept feeling the weight of the cat on my feet. Kept preparing myself to see it. Eventually I went to the lounge and watched bad karate movies with the sound turned off. Smoking one cigarette after another until there were none left. Drinking tepid tap water to get rid of the taste.

I fell asleep on the couch. The morning light wakes me as it streams through the open curtains of the lounge. No matter how wretched I feel, I can appreciate that it is a beautiful day. We have not had much of a winter. Soon we will have water restrictions.

The mountain is green. I notice this as I take De Waal Drive to the hospital. This drive is becoming routine to me; I could do it in my sleep. Still, every time I turn off from the highway, my stomach flips and I get the irrational fear that I am in the wrong lane.

The doctors are busy with her when I arrive. This too is routine. They walk in smiling, laughing, probably discussing the weekend ahead. So at ease around all this illness. When they see me, they become abashed, almost guilty. Their faces grim and once more professional. I walk out, not coping with their discomfiture. I remind myself that this is a teaching hospital: many of them are young, or at least younger than me.

One of the nurses comes up to me while I wait outside the door to my mother's room. "You seem to have a problem with death," the sister murmurs, distracting me from my thoughts. "Have you spoken to anyone?"

"No," I reply. Noncommittal.

"I can give you the number of a grief counsellor. Maybe talking to someone will help."

I take the number, to be polite, but know that I will not be making the call. As I walk away, I nearly blurt out the truth. I nearly tell her how I long for this all to end. And how I hate myself for it. Because, for my wish to come true, my mother has to die. I want to think that my desire is to alleviate her suffering, but deep within myself, I know that it is my own pain I want to relieve.

I don't know how much longer I can keep on at this. It is so hard. I feel so grown-up and alone. I wish that I had some kind of religion. That I could believe that everything happens for a reason, and that there is a better place out there. I need something to believe in. Anything but this void.

I long to talk about frivolous things. Have shallow thoughts. I want to wake up without the feeling of dread that today could be the day.

Lost in the dark

Death is everywhere around me, yet I have never noticed it. I never knew that its chilling fingers are waiting to grab hold of any likely victim. And that no one is safe. No one is untouched.

I am driving home through an unseasonable storm. I force myself to be alert, as I am tired and the road is dark. My wipers are hardly effective. A few weeks ago, I noticed that they needed replacing, but it slipped my mind. Anyway, winter was a year away. We had survived winter.

My mind wanders so easily now, but I force myself to concentrate. Still, I nearly miss it: the blinding yellow light up ahead.

Surely it's not a roadblock, I think grimly. Those lights are blue.

As I edge closer, I see the wreck. A tow truck is already on the scene with furiously flashing lights, like a rapacious lion baring its fangs and greedily smacking its lips at its prey. In the distance I hear the frenzied roar of an approaching ambulance.

I nearly stop when I see them. A young man with a cellphone attached forlornly to his ear, while his other hand grips the hand of the battered female body lying on the side of the road. As my headlights illuminate this scene, I can see the snail tracks of tears on his contorted face. He is so young; a boy really.

I wish that I had the courage to stop my car and offer assistance. Anything. I feel so inadequate. All my reserves are spent.

Then it strikes me how fleeting life can be. Death is no sometime stranger; it is all around.

As I drive home blindly, scenarios play in my head. They were a young couple, maybe childhood sweethearts, out celebrating a birthday, a graduation or a new job, when they hit the pole. Maybe they were arguing and he never saw it until it was too late; or maybe he'd had too much to drink and will never be able to live with his guilt. They had had hopes for a future and thought that their young bodies were invincible. They had had dreams of being together forever; now this will forever bind them.

I think of all the sick and dying people I pass every day at the hospital and do not see. Absorbed as I am in my own fear and grief. How many mothers have to watch over their ailing children? How many husbands have to watch their wives decline? How many children have to keep vigil over their dying parents? I am not unique, not special. I console myself that at least what I am going through is the natural order: children should outlive their parents.

When I finally make it home, I throw myself on the cold couch and bury my head in a cushion. I cry for that young life on the side of the road, which I know is no more. I cry for the seemingly unscathed young man whose life will never be the same. I cry for the girl's parents who will wake up to the news, whether by a telephone call or the untimely ringing of a doorbell. But mainly, I cry for myself. I have been so blind.

Mysterious ways

The next morning, I wake up stiff and cold from again sleeping on the couch. As I walk to the kitchen to boil water for some much-needed coffee, I look out of my window. It is a clear day outside, with no trace of last night's storm. How quickly things return to normal.

I breathe deeply as I wait for the kettle to boil, open a window and sniff the fresh morning air. The world smells clean and new – the only indication of the rain of the night before. This morning, I will take my time. I drink my coffee and manage to eat some toast. I stand in the shower and let the pulsing water revive my senses. Who is this person staring back at me in the mirror?

I am the same, yet I am forever changed. My face is the face of a woman. My eyes are wiser. It has nothing to do with the dark circles under them, which I am told can easily be cured by the new miracle cream it was my job to convince the masses to try. In fact, if I scratch around, I am sure I can find the generous sample I was given so that I could "live with the product". This is how Lili finds me when she rings the doorbell: in a towel with cream under my eyes.

"I had to come," she says, frowning at the sight of me. "I've spoken to the doctor and he says it could be any day now."

I don't remember giving her the doctor's details. But before I can say anything, my sister, my big sister, throws her arms around me and we cling to each other, towel and all.

"I meant to call you sooner," I say guiltily. "I just never had the chance." I lie. It was my own cowardice that stopped me. As long as I did not make that call, I still had hope, no matter how fragile or unrealistic.

Now, with Lili here, I feel as if I can let go just a little bit. I have had enough of being strong. I also know that it really is only for a little while longer.

"Let me get dressed," I tell her. "We can ride together. Why didn't you call? I could have fetched you from the airport."

"Ag, my company will pay for the car rental – and anyway, I left a message on your phone."

When I am dressed and my hair hastily dried, Lili looks at me and says, "You're looking good, you've lost a lot of weight."

The ride to the hospital takes longer than ever. And it's not because Lili insists on driving the hired car there. She asks about our mother, the real, gritty stuff, and apologises for not being there like she should have. "I admit, I don't deal well with these things; but you were always so strong, Danny."

I nod, and then she surprises me: "You must hate me. I've been so selfish. The truth is, I've been having some issues of my own. I have something to tell you – maybe then you'll understand." She looks at me, as if to check that I'm listening. "I'm pregnant," she announces.

I am startled – this is not what I expected from my organised sister. I didn't know she was seeing anyone special. She never mentioned anyone.

"How far are you?"

"Two months."

"And the father?" I ask. "How long have you known him?"

"Oh Danny, he's so unsuitable. He's younger than me, in fact he's still studying, but I like him. And of course I'm going to keep the baby!"

I am happy for her and tell her so. Then I laugh, "Wouldn't Mom have hated becoming a grandmother? And you're not married!"

Soberly, in mock horror, we say in chorus: "What would the neighbours say?"

Driving to the hospital, for what may very well be the last time, the two of us are convulsed with laughter. We laugh so much that the tears stream down our faces, ruining my earlier eye-care and Lili's carefully applied mascara. I am sure that it is the first time that either of us has laughed, really laughed, in months.

Suddenly, I recall something my mother told me a long, long time ago: "When one life ends, another begins."

Isn't life strange?

Summer 1985

Summer explodes upon us. The heat from the sun stuns us as we shed our jerseys and blankets. Soon it will be time for the beach. Christmas is around the corner and, before long, I will help Ma make the Christmas puddings. I have started saving up silver five-cent pieces in preparation. I cannot wait to make my wish. I know what I will be wishing for, but I cannot say or else it won't come true.

We have finished our exams and are waiting for our reports. We know that many high-school students did not write exams this year. What is going to happen to them? The Casspirs were parked outside the high school opposite our school until the schools closed for the holiday. They never wrote exams, Lili told me. Next year, she is supposed to go to that school and she is worried.

Our mother is worried too. Worried that the classes will be too big. Worried that Lili will get involved in things that she is too young to understand.

We are always worried. Worried about money. Worried about our mother's job. Worried about what is happening in the country.

We are not sure about Christmas this year. We still haven't heard from our father, although Uncle Charlie came to visit our mother once.

I wanted to ask him about my father and if he still saw him, but he and my mother sat in the lounge and closed the door.

I wonder if our father will come around to wish us. I think of all the presents he will bring. But Christmas passes without a visit – not even a telephone call. Our Matthews grandparents don't call us either, but we don't mind. On Christmas day, our mother says we can sleep as late as we want, since we do not have to go to church. There is no question about it: we are eating with Ma this year. We pull our crackers and stuff ourselves on turkey and trifle and no one mentions last year's disastrous Christmas at Ma and Pa Matthews' house. Not even me.

And although I miss my father, sometimes I'm glad that he is gone. Sometimes the air is so light in the house, I feel like laughing. Our mother sings old love songs from when she was younger. When "her" songs come on the radio, she'll grab me or Lili and teach us how to jazz. At times like these, we do fun things only, like go to the movies or bake. Biscuits, bread, cake. And not only on a Sunday – whenever the fancy strikes our mother. She makes the best coconut loaf cake. We eat it hot out of the tin. She cuts thick slices. Lili and I stand around her, waiting for our pieces as the fragrance of the warm coconut tempts us. We don't bother with plates. It is so hot, the cake crumbles in our hands as we try to lift it to our mouths. It burns our lips and tongues, but we eat it until there is only a heel left.

Cool in a crisis

The nurses' faces are grim as we approach the nurses' station. They are as solicitous as ever, showing compassion for what we are going through.

The doctor greets us at the door and shakes his head. "You must prepare yourselves for the worst," he says.

I know that they tell the family this only when it is the end.

Lili and I walk into the room. The only sign that our mother is still alive is the laboured breathing of the respirator. We look at each other, resigned, unable to voice what we are feeling. As I look at the helpless body lying prone on the bed, I think to myself that this is not my mother. This is not living. My mother was always such a vibrant person. Even in her darkest moments, she would have her exultant highs. Highs that the two of us standing here learnt to fear, as they were a precursor to her lows. And her lows were dismally low.

I stand back, allowing Lili to survey her. Involuntarily, Lili takes a sharp intake of breath as she sees our mother. This stranger. No regret could sway us to pray for a miracle now. It would be too selfish. We know that we must let her go.

We sit on either side of the bed. Not saying much. Or at least, I don't.

Lili leans close to our mother's face, murmuring secrets, making promises. So much to say – and yet it is not important any more.

I look at my mother and see that her suffering has written itself on her body, on her face. She is a ghost of herself. There is no trace of her beauty, of the vitality that was once our mother. How she would have hated to see herself like this! I am glad for the small mercy of her coma.

"When did she become so old?" Lili asks me.

She is not old. Her body appears shrunken and emaciated, as small as a little girl's.

Why must she suffer so?

Waiting for the night to fall

There is nothing more that we can do. We know this. Any action on our part is superfluous and unnecessary. There is nothing that we can do to help her. We are no longer our mother's caretakers. All we can do is be here. Maybe that is all we could ever do.

As the day progresses, our mother's skin turns cold, her lips blue. Her breath becomes shallower and shallower. Still, she breathes. We are sure that today will be the day. We are too afraid to leave the room, so we do not eat. Once or twice, I sneak out for a guilty cigarette. I come back in as soon as I am finished, and vigorously scrub my hands with the detergent at the small basin in the corner of the room.

The nurses pop in occasionally to check our mother's breathing; they look at her cursorily and at us more searchingly. "Are you the only family?" they ask. Lili and I nod distractedly. We do not want to invite anyone here on this day. We will not allow our mother to become a spectacle.

Outside, dusk falls through the high hospital windows. Lights are being switched on in the city as people come home from work, suppers are made and children greeted. An ordinary day. A day like any other.

A nurse comes in and switches on a light. Soon it will be visiting hours for the patients in the wards outside. I tell Lili what to expect. The sympathy and the compassion, which is all these strangers can give, all I will accept. I tell her about the prayer groups – of all religions and denominations. I tell of the prayers that have been going out into the heavens for our mother since she has been lying here.

Lili says, "I wish I'd brought a Bible so I could read to her," and I frown, surprised at the sentiment.

All day, there is no dramatic change. The decline is gradual; with each slow minute, we resign ourselves and steel ourselves for the inevitable.

Some of the regular visitors knock lightly on the door and ask me how my mother is doing. They smile when I introduce Lili; tell me that they can see the resemblance. A Moslem lady whose daughter is in for some or other minor operation brings me a plate of samoosas that she made herself, she tells me. I thank her and take the plate, but neither Lili nor I can eat. The samoosas go cold; the crisp pastry soggy.

Then visiting hour is over. A relative quiet descends. Medication is administered for the night. The patients succumb to the twilight of sleep. The few who can walk stand outside the door, but do not come in. Curious, though sensitive to our feelings. Everyone shares our sense of foreboding.

It is dark now; we cannot see anything out of the window except the colourful lights of Cape Town and the stars in the sky. I feel like a sleep-walker. I imagine that this is happening to someone else. Lili is mutter-ing long-forgotten psalms under her breath. The air is static, charged. And as we sit, the respirator starts to whine and wail.

Will the crowd disperse?

The attending doctor rushes in, a resident in tow, followed by what seems like all the nurses on the floor. Lili makes way as the doctors push past her. I walk over to her side, the side nearest the door, and we clutch each other's hands.

Is this the end? Is this how the story plays out?

A nurse with a kind, round face ushers us outside and waits with us while the others are busy with my mother. After an age, the doctors troop out, and by the way they meet our eyes, we know that there has been a temporary reprieve.

"You can go back inside," the tired young doctor says, "it was nothing."

But the older nurse tells us, "Why don't you girls get some rest? I'll take you to a private room, where you can be alone. Mummy's okay for now. I'll call you if you need to come."

Reassured, we mechanically follow her to the windowless waiting room. We pass another family, anxiously pacing the area outside the general ward. They too have a mother in here. Soon they too will be ushered to a private room. It is inevitable. We exchange grey smiles in recognition of this. There are so many of them. Lili and I have only each other.

The air in the room is stale and heavy with shed and unshed tears. Thick with all the fears attendant on such a place. Still, it is a respite from my mother's bedside. The nurse says that she will wait with my mother and call us if there is any need.

Lili arranges herself in the yellow leatherette chair and closes her eyes. Did she really arrive from London this morning only? How has she managed to stay awake so long? I push two worn beige chairs together, but it doesn't work. There is no way for me to get comfortable, so after a while, I go outside for another cigarette.

Silent all these years

"Do you remember that time . . . in the hospital?"

The question floats and hangs suspended between us. Lili looks at me. She does not answer. We need no words. We remember.

You can remain silent only in the company of those you truly love.

248

No need to analyse. To explain. To fill the void with unnecessary words. To remember is enough. This we know. And we have been prepared for this day. As long as memory, we have been prepared.

It seems as if it has always been the three of us. Me, my mother and Lili. My friends used to marvel at how close we were, but it is the closeness of survival. It is like being taught a sacred truth, and then realising that what you were taught is no truth.

There was no hint of what was to come. If there was, we chose to ignore it. Children can be so determinedly optimistic. As a child, you create your own reality. Later the real reality comes crashing in, forcing you to own up to what you'd rather not see.

Afterwards, it felt like a hurricane had blown through our lives; we were uprooted, devastated, yet alive. Ultimately wiser. Wise enough to know that you cannot fashion your own truths.

We were ever preoccupied with our mother's death. In her darkest days, our mother would tell us: "I don't think I will live to see the end of the year." The two of us would be horrified – we seriously believed our mother's proclamations. I would bawl and Lili, being older and being Lili, would choke back a whimper, her eyes shining. We would tell her hysterically how we could not live without her. Beg her not to leave us. But we were smart. Once she had told us this too often, we began to relax. The threat began to lose its terror.

Except it wasn't always a threat.

Summer 1986

Summer draws to a lazy close. This is my favourite time of year, the end of summer. After a while, the intense heat of the middle of summer becomes oppressive. My body feels sticky and clammy sitting in class in January. In February the sun is gentler.

Yes, Lili and I are back at school, back at home, back to normal. I like my new teacher, and I am looking forward to the year ahead. Lili has started high school near Ma's house and takes a bus all by herself to get there. The Standard Six class of the school opposite was too full, our mother said, what with the new intake and the Standard Sixes of last year in one class.

Our mother has found yet another new job in an office in Town and is settling in. She passed her matric exams and talks about enrolling at Unisa to do a BA – in Art. Our country seems to be settling down too. Ma tells us that Auntie Astrid wants her to visit her in Canada, and she wants to go. We are looking ahead, and tell one another hopefully that this year will be better than the last one. And we don't mention my father.

The only change is the paintings. Angry, lurid smears on canvases that seem to overwhelm our house, spilling out of the lounge and into the other rooms with their grinning images of chaos and blood. They mean nothing more than a nuisance, a slight irritation when we bash our bare legs against the wooden frames. During the time we lived with Ma, Lili and I have learnt to relax our vigilance. We are all okay.

This time of year is special for another reason: it is hanepoot season, which lasts a few weeks only. My mother only eats hanepoot grapes. We drive around to find the best specimens, which turn out to be on a farm in Constantia. The farmer allows the public into his vineyard to pick the grapes themselves – you pay per kilo. What fun we have! We wipe the grapes clean between our fingers and thumbs and eat them right there in the vineyard. They are still warm from the sun and indescribably sweet. We end up buying boxes and boxes of grapes. The car is full, the boxes balanced next to me on the back seat jostling for space. Lili, as the eldest, gets to sit in front.

"What are we going to do with all of these grapes?" Lili asks, concerned.

No matter how much we love grapes, it would take the three of us weeks to get through all of these. My mother purses her lips in concentration, as if it occurred to her now only; then brightly, like a woman with a plan, she says, "We'll stop over by Ma on the way back and give her some. Then maybe – who knows – if there's more left over we'll tramp the grapes and make wine."

"Really?" I ask, intrigued.

Lili just rolls her eyes and looks at me. Dummy.

The next night is a night like any other. Our mother comes home soon after six, gingerly steps out of her high heels and stalks the house in her pantyhose.

"Dish up for yourselves," she instructs us as she puts the pot of last night's curry on the stove to heat up. "Lili, make sure the pot doesn't burn. I'm going to take a bath."

Lili and I mutter and complain. It is too hot for curry. There is nothing worse than having to eat last night's supper – but we know better than to say anything. Humming softly and tunelessly, my mother runs the bath. Scalding hot, the way she likes it.

After supper, Lili and I clean the kitchen and discuss our mother's birthday, which is a few weeks away. It is her first birthday since our father left, and we think of ways to make it special. I wonder whether our father will come around for her birthday, but I don't ask Lili. Instead, I ask her what she thinks we should buy our mother with the money we've been saving.

Lili shrugs. "We should ask Mommy," she says. "That way, we'll know she likes it." She calls, "Mommy, what do you want for Christmas this year?"

No answer.

"Mommy . . .?"

We look at each other.

"Maybe she's washing her hair and can't hear," I suggest. Our mother likes to wash her hair in the bath.

"Yes," Lili agrees. "I'll go ask her."

I follow Lili to the bathroom.

"Mommy?" Lili taps on the door. "Danny and I want to know what you want for Christmas."

This is strange. Our mother is silent.

Lili tries to push the door, but a towel is wedged underneath, making it impossible to open. The key has been missing for a few months now, but we no longer troop into the bathroom like we used to. We are learning to respect one another's need for privacy. But this is different.

"Mom!"

Steam escapes through the crack in the door. We cannot see anything in the dark, misted-up bathroom.

"Danny! Help me!" Lili yells urgently. "Help me get this door open!"

Together we push until the door gives way. The steam clings to the garish turquoise tiles, forming sweaty beads on the shiny surface. Our mother's face is motionless as she lies back in the bath, but her luminous flesh rises and falls, rises and falls, almost imperceptibly.

"Switch on the light!" Lili shouts. "Mom!"

All I can see is the red. The rosy pink-red of the bath water, the orange-red splotches on the turquoise tiles and on the yellow enamel of the bath. The screaming reds rush and swirl in front of my eyes as I fall.

I don't know how Lili manages, but she does. She staunches our mother's drip-dripping wrists with the towel, and manages to call for help.

I wake up on the plastic runner that covers the carpet in the passage outside the bathroom. Lili looks up and blankly tells me to hold the towel in place. I ask no questions. I just obey.

Ma arrives at the same time as the ambulance. Her face has lost all of its colour. She suddenly looks like an old, old woman. She bundles me aside to make way for the paramedics, shielding my eyes with her hands. Lili tries to shield my mother's dignity with hers.

The neighbours' eyes are keenly focused on our house as they stand on their stoeps. The bolder ones mill as close to the ambulance as is decent. The ambulancemen allow Lili to ride in the back with our mother. Ma and I follow in the big Valiant.

When we reach the hospital, Lili is standing in front of the emergency room. A plump, young nurse is trying to console her. Lili brushes her off rudely when she sees us. Ma speaks to the nurses while the two of us, Lili and I, hold each other. We are two little girls lost in a grown-up world.

None of us ever speak about that night again. Not Lili, not my mother, not Ma. Not me.

Aftershock

Although my mother survived and we survived, I knew that none of us would ever be the same again. In my core, I knew that I would forever be responsible for my mother's well-being. Who is it who said, if you save someone's life you become responsible for that life? I took my responsibilities seriously.

As soon as she could, Lili moved away from home. First to Rhodes University in Grahamstown, then out of the country altogether. Like Astrid, Lili found her wings and flew away. Although she returned to the country from time to time, she never lived in Cape Town again.

I remember that night in the hospital. Lili and I were waiting alone as the darkest of night became morning. Ma was off somewhere, checking on our mother's condition. For a while, it was hanging in the balance – she had lost so much blood. Sitting in the waiting room, I prayed and prayed, begging God not to take our mother away from us.

Lili sat rigidly in her chair, staring ahead, her eyes not meeting mine. Neither of us slept at all. I don't know if Lili prayed. When the morning came, Ma came to call us. She told us that we were allowed to go into the room to see our mother, even though she was sleeping.

I was so relieved. I could expel all the stale breath that had been collecting in my chest. Lili pulled away. She refused to see our mother. Her face was pale, but her eyes blazed. "I'll wait in the car, if you don't mind, Ma," she said politely.

Then she walked away.

Sadness

My mother was discharged from the hospital. We pretended that what had happened had never happened. With the pretence came a semblance of relief. I went back to my school and Lili went back to hers. Our mother returned to work. Ma cancelled her trip to Canada.

Later, when our mother started seeing a psychologist, Lili and I allowed ourselves to have some hope. Then she stopped going to the sessions. We didn't know this until the psychologist turned up at our house one Saturday morning. I was a bit surprised, but not overly concerned. Some people are really dedicated to their jobs, I rationalised.

They sat in the lounge with the door closed for more than two hours. I remember this because I thought it was strange that my mother didn't offer him something to drink in all that time. Not that I was going to disturb them!

Our mother's face was inscrutable when she let him out. Lili and I buzzed around her nervously. As his car pulled away, she slammed the front door shut with surprising violence.

"Bloody interfering so-and-so," she raged. "How dare he?"

"What did he want?" Lili asked with studied nonchalance.

"He wanted to know why I stopped coming to see him. But I don't need his help any more. I am fine. I promise."

Lili and I looked at her, unable to hide our scepticism. We wanted to believe that she was as fine as she said she was. We could not force her to attend her counselling. Instead, we watched her vigilantly.

Come undone

Seeing my mother miserable was like seeing her reflected in water or through a thick piece of glass. I wanted to reach her, but she evaded me. All I could do was watch and witness. Remonstration would not reach her. If I tried to raise my concerns, ask her if she needed to see someone, she'd look at me keenly, as if I didn't know what I was talking about. Or bewildered – as if I did not know what I was talking about.

A succession of uncles started streaming into our lives. Of course we rebelled. I think a childish part of me clung to the hope that my father would return and that things would be different this time. Eventually, I stopped dreaming about the impossible. I grew up and left home, though I was never far. Always watching. I learnt to ride things out. A quaint euphemism. I learnt to anticipate the worst. Always pre-empting bad news. But the spectre of the phone call or the knock at my door late at night never lost its dread.

Driving to visit her, before turning my car into her road, I'd freeze for a nanosecond, and call to mind the scene that possibly awaited me. Flashing lights, an ambulance, the police, curious neighbours. Irrational but real fears. Then, when I arrived at her house and everything appeared fine and my fears unfounded, I would be overcome with a profound sense of relief. As if my fears had had substance after all.

I obsessed about my mother's death way, way before I had any real reason to fear. I would tread around her, trying to smooth out her life though I could not smooth out her moods. Because I never knew what she was capable of when she was down, it became preferable that she wasn't too up, either. What's the saying – what goes up must come down?

Now I know that not knowing is worse than knowing. Now that my biggest fear is going to be realised, I learn this truth. I am not sure when, exactly, but I know that her death is imminent. It is highly likely that I will outlive her, save for a freak accident or a terrorist attack.

Yet I have not fallen apart. I have not come undone.

Praying for time

In the morning, before I am aware of it, slowly, gently, the hospital starts to stir. In the distance, I hear the echo of a flushing toilet, breaking the spell of my remembering and reminding me of where I am. My mouth tastes stale and bitter from all the coffee and cigarettes. Lili is not in the room, which is strange, since I never noticed her leaving.

I find it difficult to rise from my chair. No one thought that my mother would survive yesterday. What will today bring?

A hesitant knock on the door startles me. I jump up guiltily. "Your aunt's here," the nursing aid informs me. Then, to explain her intrusion, she adds, "Sister said you'd be awake." Relieved, I thank her, knowing that she could have told me something worse.

I scratch in my bag for a piece of chewing gum to mask my morning breath. Pat my hair back and try to unrumple my tracksuit. Taking a deep breath, I walk towards my mother's room.

Lili is sitting in the same chair as yesterday. Astrid and a plainer, more soberly dressed woman stand at the foot of the bed.

My mother looks more and more like a little girl. Her face is smoother than it has been for a long time. The suffering of the last few months seems to be erasing itself from her face. I alone know that she has suffered. And fought.

Then it hits me. Perhaps my mother had to learn the value of life – to know what it means to struggle for every breath. We all take life so lightly, yet we are in awe of death. Are our lives so far removed from death that we contemplate our mortality only when we are forced to do so? When we can no longer run away from the fact that everyone must die?

Surreptitiously, I glance at the clock. Not yet six o'clock, and yet Astrid is immaculately dressed and made up. Not a hair out of place, her sig–

nature red lipstick painted on carefully. Looking like she just walked out of a beauty salon.

"Darling," she exclaims, "I couldn't sleep all night! I just got a feeling that I had to come here this morning. Why didn't you call me?"

I cannot explain to her how I have merely been functioning the past few days. How I've had no time to think of decorum. There is no guide on how to behave in times like these. So instead, I smile sheepishly at her and the strange woman.

"Oops, where's my manners?" Astrid trills. "I've asked my minister to pray for May. Danika, this is Reverend Elizabeth Cloete."

"Pleased to meet you," I murmur as the woman clasps my hand in both of hers.

Why didn't I think of this? I ask myself. But my mother has never been religious. I doubt that she went to one church service since my father left, other than the occasional wedding or funeral she was obliged to attend.

"Would you like to pray?" Reverend Cloete asks, and the four of us hold hands as we stand around my mother's bed in the quiet of the morning. Praying for her soul to find peace.

Tears in my hand

After the prayer, a calmness descends. I am convinced that there is a light form at the head of my mother's bed. I am not a religious woman, yet still I feel it. I know that I must let my mother go. Finally I am ready. This can no longer be about me. What kind of monster would I be to want to keep her alive?

I have accepted that the doctors can do no more for her. All I can hope for is that she is not afraid. Lili and I take up our positions on either side of her, holding her icy hands in ours. Her breath flutters like the merest butterfly wings. The spaces between her breaths grow and grow so that, automatically, we each hold our breath until she takes the next one. Then she doesn't.

I stare at her, unsure if this is what I think it is. Waiting for the inevitable next breath. I take it back, I am not ready! No one can ever be ready for this!

Seconds pass, then a full minute, all of us not daring to exhale. Eventually, the reverend breaks the spell and calls the nurse. It is over.

♠

Mechanically, I do the things that people do at times like these. Wait for the attending doctors to check on her for the last time and write their reports so that they can close the file. I scream inside as the doctor writes "DECEASED" on the cover of her folder. In glaring, indelible red ink.

Astrid starts phoning around for an undertaker and asks the good reverend whether she will officiate at the burial. Wheels, set in motion, turn smoothly. Millions of people have done this before me. And people cope. Still, I cannot let go. I cannot let my mother go. I clutch her fingers and smooth back her hair.

Tenderly, Lili disengages my fingers, kneels next to my chair and hugs me. We hold each other, frozen in time. United in our grief.

After forever, Lili pulls away and looks at me. "Take my car and go home," she tells me. "Have a shower, rest for a while . . . I'll wait here."

Emotionally and physically spent, I don't argue. As I turn away, she whispers, "Thank you."

Somehow I make it to the car, through the labyrinthine hospital. The day is still fresh and new. For most people the day has not yet started. As I drive home in the unfamiliar car, I notice that the traffic is picking up in the opposite direction. It is peak hour. As the rental car eats up the open road, I envy those people stuck in traffic. Their frantic, untouched lives. The more I think about it, the more I cry.

I yearn to find traces of myself, but I am nowhere. I am everywhere. My heart throbs and explodes and bursts. My limbs are heavy, liquid, rooted; but I am flying. Pieces of me shatter in the burgeoning light. Is this what freedom feels like?

All at once the universe makes sense for me; for a brief moment I understand everything. Yet I wish that I do not know. Oh, for the comfort of ignorance – it is bliss. This is unbliss.

I know that my mother has found peace at last. That she has gone to a better place, and all the other platitudes. It does not stop the tears. Or the pain. I drive through my tears, anxious to get home.

I don't know how I manage to get home, but I do. Somehow, we always make it home. Once inside the door of my flat, my legs crumple and I fall to the ground, prostrate with my grief. From my vantage point on the floor, I realise: when someone you love dies, part of your heart dies too. I cry for the death of my heart. The piece that will forever be lost to any person washed up on its shore. I cry for the girl I was and the woman I have become. I cry for the girl-woman who is no more and the salvation that will never come.

Some people are numbed by emotion. I am not such a person. I clutch my hands to my face and sob. Finally spent, I look at my hands and I realise that pain, too, is tangible. Nothing more than the tears in my hands.

This is home

Slowly, Lili and I walk to the gate of our mother's house. Anxious not to catch the attention of any of the neighbours, who are eager to press their sympathy on us. There is a pallor of neglect, of sadness about the house. I have not come here as often as I should have.

"Is it September already?" I mutter, half to Lili and half to myself, as I notice the Cape may petals strewn like confetti on the ground. Lili looks at the tree at the side of the house, but doesn't answer. She turns the key into the front door, then steps back, hesitant.

"It's fine," I tell her, not feeling fine but trying to fill the moment with words. "I've been here a few times since . . . you know, Mom went to hospital."

The stuffiness in the house is overwhelming. I choke on it. As I open the curtains and windows, I take in big gulps of fresh air. How do you pack up a life? How do you decide what is important and what is not?

My mother's very essence lingers throughout the house. Her paintings on the walls, our photographs. There is no place she has not touched. I am sure if I hold her pillow to my face, I will smell her. Like she was before. Before she became the dying woman.

In the bathroom, there is a dried-out piece of soap in the shower.

The towels are clean, if a bit musty. Lili gets to work, sorting out what we will give to the homeless shelter and what must be thrown away. Soon her carrier bags are full. Then the cleaning materials in her arsenal come out. She furiously attacks the tiles, the shower door, the drip tray. She squirts detergents into the toilet bowl and under the rim. I know that she will go down on her hands and knees to scrub the floor and I want to tell her to be careful – for the baby – but I know that this is something she must get out of her system.

I find myself in the back yard. It is an unruly riot of colour. For a moment, I am reminded of one of my mother's canvases. There are variegated tulips, purple-blue irises with their bright yellow beards and daffodils, some withering away, others coming into bloom. And masses of her favourite ranunculi and sweet-smelling freesias in containers.

"How did they survive?" I wonder aloud. "With so little water . . ." I remember my mother telling me that bulbs must always be wet in order to flower.

Then I realise. They survived because they had to. Sometimes we can grow without nurturing. Growing just because we can and we must.

I snip off a glorious lilac freesia, breathing the perfume in deeply and twirling the stem in my hand as I marvel at the tiny trumpet flower. I imagine my mother looking at her garden and smiling her approval. Her joy in something as small as her garden in bloom.

"Lili," I call, "you have to see this!"

Don't speak

Absentmindedly, Lili and I pull at the weeds choking the plants in the container. The discarded weeds form an untidy pile on the moss-spattered paving. The silence is interrupted by the cheerful twittering of the birds congregating inquisitively on the telephone wire above. Our neighbourhood has grown quiet. All the children have grown up and moved away, as have we. This is an ageing neighbourhood. Young people don't buy houses in these areas any more. The resale value is low, I hear.

As we weed, the flickering images of another time dance before us. We each have our own memories, our own pictures. Eventually, Lili breaks the reverie. "Let's finish up," she says, "it's getting cold."

We have so much to do before Lili returns to her life in London.

"I'll clean the studio," I tell her. A while ago, my mother converted my and Lili's room into a studio. Evidently the light was good there, too. Her paintings, the ones she didn't sell, are lined up against the wall. There are so few of them.

I open the cupboards, eager to see whether she kept any of my old clothes. My mother was not the sentimental type. She would have donated the clothes to people who came to the door with hard-luck stories or offers of trade. Cheap ceramic ornaments in exchange for your old clothes. The few old clothes are obviously just things she forgot to give away or which discerning beggars had refused. There are also old shoes.

How my mother loved her shoes! Some of them are still in their original boxes. I squat down to open the boxes.

The top boxes contain shoes, but when I reach the bottom box, an old-fashioned hatbox, I realise that it contains my mother's memories. When she was dying, I briefly considered putting together such a box for her, like they do for Aids patients now, but decided against it. I thought that my mother would take offence at the suggestion.

Curiosity gets the better of me. I rifle idly through this Pandora's box. There are a few of the black hard-cover books, some sketches and a mishmash of photographs. It is the first photograph that strikes me.

There we are, smiling our toothpaste grins into the camera: my mother, my father, Lili and myself. Resplendent in colour. It is the kind of photograph that certain families now have made into Christmas cards, with syrupy messages that contain updates on the year's happenings.

We are sitting on the couch. Before the brown velvet became faded by the sun and worn thin in places. My father is wearing a brown sports jacket and pants, my mother the kind of dress favoured by Princess Diana around the time of William's birth. The ones with the wide, white collars. Lili and I are dressed in identical dresses, although hers is pink and mine is blue. It was always that way, even though I preferred pink; our colours were staked out for us from birth, I guess. Lili is about nine and I am about four.

The family seems so hopeful and new. My fingers caress the shiny surface of the photograph, touching each one of us briefly, tenderly. What happened to us?

Tucked in amongst the photographs is a postcard invitation to the opening of the first exhibition that my mother was part of. She sold her first painting that day. The exhibition was supposedly one of female struggle artists. The premise was obviously that they were doubly challenged. It was one of the few highlights of her artistic career. A career that never reached the heights she'd hoped for.

"I never thought I'd see this day," she confided to Lili and me.

What a laugh she had at the expense of her fellow artists. Preparing for the installation, she would regale us with her descriptions of them. "Why do these women think they have to look unattractive in order to be taken seriously? They don't shave their legs, or wear make-up. Can you believe it?"

Lili was home for the holidays from Grahamstown. She had a Feminism elective, and winced at my mother's politically incorrect talk.

The two of us marvelled at our mother's place in such a crowd. She was always immaculately groomed. When we were growing up, she taught us that a lady never left the house without her best face on. Grooming was important, she said.

Flushed with the success of her first sale, she took Lili and me out to afternoon tea at the Mount Nelson. We looked very grown-up in our high heels and lipsticked mouths. Celebrating. Our mother forced us to try everything, determined to get her money's worth.

A group of tourists was seated at the next table. Our mother embarrassed us by smiling and trilling her voice in their direction until one of the men came over. How she giggled like a little girl when the man used the cliché of calling her our sister. Lili and I rolled our eyes as we faded into the background of our mother's brilliance.

Now that I think about it, our mother was so young, I guess she could have passed for her daughters' sister. When the man found out what we were celebrating, he ordered a bottle of champagne for our table. Real champagne. Just like in the movies.

I turn my attention to the books. I flip through the first one, without reading. A diary of sorts. It seems that my mother recorded every year of her adult life. Her small, cramped writing covers the pages. It is not the flamboyant writing that you would expect from an artist.

I can read these, I think. I can learn the truth and answer the questions that have plagued me all this while. But whose truth would it be? Who says that knowledge is power?

I know what I must do. What my mother would want me to do. Gathering up the diaries, I carry them outside.

From the bathroom, Lili calls, "Where are you going?"

"I'm getting rid of the weeds," I answer.

Closing my eyes against the sudden burst of sunlight that floods the garden as the clouds shift, it comes to me. I do not need a Rosetta stone to unravel the mysteries of my mother. After all, I am no archae-ologist and her life is not a ruin. Perhaps my truth is all I need. And my memories.

I find my mother's spade and, with a spurt of renewed energy, I start to dig.

MAXINE CASE was born in Cape Town and has been a voracious reader from a young age. She has worked in publishing for a number of years.

All We Have Left Unsaid is her first novel. It won the Commonwealth Writers' Prize for Best First Book in Africa in 2007.